*Shooting the Fox*

T0287407

Also by Marion Halligan

*Valley of Grace*
*The Apricot Colonel*
*Murder on the Apricot Coast*
*The Taste of Memory*
*The Point*
*The Fog Garden*
*The Golden Dress*
*Cockles of the Heart*
*Wishbone*
*The Worry Box*
*Lovers' Knots*
*Eat My Words*
*Spider Cup*
*The Hanged Man in the Garden*
*The Living Hothouse*
*Self Possession*
*The Widwife's Daughters* (for children)
*Out of the Picture*
*Collected Stories*
*Those Women Who Go to Hotels* (with Lucy Frost)

# MARION HALLIGAN

# *Shooting the Fox*

ALLEN&UNWIN

**Previous publication:** 'Shooting the fox', *Island Magazine*; 'Valiant', *Best Australian Stories 2003* (Black Inc.); 'The train crossed a bridge', *Australian Literary Review*, *Best Australian Stories 2009* (Black Inc.); 'The white peacock', *Best Australian Stories 2008* (Black Inc.); 'A grove of olives', *Griffith Review*; 'At the end of no line', *Southerly*; 'What about the spider?', *Meanjin*; 'It's the cheroot', *New Australian Stories* (Scribe); 'The original is unfaithful to the translation', *Meanjin*; 'Polyhymnia', *Muse Magazine*; 'Irregular verbs', *Penguin Australian Summer Stories*; 'Letters from Eden', *Meanjin* (as 'Epistles from Eden').

First published in 2011

Copyright © Marion Halligan 2011

All rights reserved. No part of this book may be reproduced or transmitted in any form or by any means, electronic or mechanical, including photocopying, recording or by any information storage and retrieval system, without prior permission in writing from the publisher. The Australian *Copyright Act 1968* (the Act) allows a maximum of one chapter or 10 per cent of this book, whichever is the greater, to be photocopied by any educational institution for its educational purposes provided that the educational institution (or body that administers it) has given a remuneration notice to Copyright Agency Limited (CAL) under the Act.

Allen & Unwin
Sydney, Melbourne, Auckland, London

83 Alexander Street
Crows Nest NSW 2065
Australia
Phone: (61 2) 8425 0100
Fax: (61 2) 9906 2218
Email: info@allenandunwin.com
Web: www.allenandunwin.com

Cataloguing-in-Publication details are available
from the National Library of Australia
www.trove.nla.gov.au

ISBN 978 1 74237 667 7

Edited by Rosanne Fitzgibbon
Internal design by Sandy Cull, gogoGingko
Set in 13/17 pt Granjon by Post Pre-press Group, Australia
Printed and bound in Australia by Griffin Press

10 9 8 7 6 5 4 3 2 1

MIX
Paper from responsible sources
FSC
www.fsc.org
FSC® C009448

The paper in this book is FSC certified.
FSC promotes environmentally responsible, socially beneficial and economically viable management of the world's forests.

*To Brenda and Rosie*

'we spend our years as a tale that is told.'
Psalm 90, 9

## SHOOTING THE FOX

Would you like to see the fox I shot this morning, he said, as he opened the gate in the wall.

This is a particular form of words. It is not a question. You do not say no. It appears to be polite—would you—but it leaves no room.

I went and saw the fox. Exquisite red creature. It does not know yet that it is dead. Its eye is not dim, its brush is defiant. Soon it will droop and decay and know its own mortality.

His name is Malcolm and he wishes to marry me. I am a forty-three-year-old virgin and my name is Gloria. An unsuitable name. Except when I sing *Gloria in excelsis Deo*. Not that I can sing. I lift up my head and open my mouth and pretend to be part of the glorious harmony of the choir. I open my mouth and no sound comes out, but the choir's sound fills it. We are very proud of the choir at my school, it is one of the things we are famous for.

The girls are cruel. Generation after generation they come and flourish and go. They can take all sorts of forms, and one of them is tropical flowers, growing lustily on their vines, their preening tendrils twining and prying, threatening to crush the frail trellis of the school between their vigorous thighs. Flowers that are creamy, rosy, dusky, thickly petalled, with long fleshy throats full of pollen. Even when they sit demurely in class, their blue-checked dresses smoothed down as far as they will go over these strong thighs, the slit between them cries out, I am open and thickly pinkly flesh, I am filled with honey, my sticky juices are waiting for the protuberances of men to find me out and fill me. It is hard to close your eyes to these shameless songs, it is necessary to say in a clear hard voice the tenses of French verbs, words without sentences to give them meaning, possessing only syntax. Pay attention, girls, it is a matter simply of rote learning, of reciting over and over until you know by heart.

Their hearts beat, the buttons of their dresses rise and fall, they slide undone to show lacy bras and the smooth flesh with these powerful hearts beating.

The verbs though meaningless alone are a spell to keep lascivious scents at bay, otherwise their languid beguiling odour-songs would drive us all mad.

Would you like to see the fox I shot this morning, Malcolm said, and I went through the gate in the wall and down to the kitchen garden, where the fox hung, its tail bushy, its pointed little face open-mouthed as if to draw in air.

I could shoot a few and make you a fur coat, he said, and I remembered women of my grandmother's age, wearing fox stoles with beady false black eyes and a little chain joining sharp-toothed mouth to legs, bony legs with padded paws. I always wondered how they could bear having a dead animal hanging round their necks. Even flattened out and lined with shiny brown satin.

Why do you shoot them? I asked Malcolm. Don't they keep the rabbits in check?

I shoot the rabbits too, he said. I am cooking rabbit stew for dinner. You'll enjoy its gamey flavour, not bland like the farmed creatures.

He is a hunter. He wants to marry me. His name is John Malcolm Crape Pembroke. I saw it in a book. I would be the third Mrs Malcolm Pembroke. Though I could keep my own name. Gloria Jones. When the girls ask me for an example of bathos I am careful not to offer my own name.

The girls call me mademoiselle. I met Malcolm when his daughter was in the boarding house. He came to see each of her teachers when he picked her up at the end of term. She was a good French scholar. Now she lives in Aix-en-Provence, studying translation. She has a brother who is a merchant banker in London.

Malcolm lives deep in the high country in a tower. It's old, built by convicts who first made the bricks. You can find arrows and marks like birds' feet, which ask you to think of the men who made them. It's like a medieval watchtower, designed to keep an eye out for marauding tribes. It is wide and tall, with one round room on each floor. In the basement is a studio, with presses and machines. Then a room with books and a harpsichord painted with blue-grey landscapes of weeping-barked eucalyptus trees. This floor is surrounded by a rim of rooms he calls his offices, a kitchen and scullery and pantry, a laundry and mudroom and storerooms, opening through arches and doors into the main room.

Upstairs is a room arranged for me, and then on the top floor his bedroom. A staircase zigzags round the walls to each floor and up through his bedroom to the battlemented roof. Last year the second Mrs Pembroke fell from this roof and died. He was away at the time. Was it an accident or did she do it on purpose? Who knows? She liked the roof and often sat on its turreted rim. She could see the bones of the garden from there, she said. So he told me.

How can I marry you, I said. I am a schoolteacher. I cannot live here and teach in my school.

I am a rich man, he said. You do not need to work.

I thought of the girls, blooming so tropically and self-regardingly, new ones year after year, hardly paying attention to the elderly virgin who teaches them French. Though they do learn the French, mostly, and pass their exams, and blow the air round my cheeks with kisses and thanks when they leave to truly blossom in the real world. Heedless they are, and cruel by nature but without malice. Could I give them up?

I did not find out then what he did for a living. Maybe I thought he was a rich man by inheritance, that the curious garden and the tower were not earned by him. I am used to rich parents at my school. Later I asked him.

I'm a writer, he said.

What of? I asked, because mostly writers I know are not rich.

When we are married I will show you, he said.

I asked if I would have seen any of his books. No, he said. I asked if he wrote under his own name. Two of them, he said. John Malcolm Crape Pembroke: I supposed his pen name would be John Crape. A strong and simple name.

I said, I am a forty-three-year-old virgin. How can you want to marry me?

People think it is difficult to manage to be a forty-three-year-old virgin in this day and age, but it hasn't been for me. It is something that happened quite naturally, and there I am sitting in my school like a rose hip on a branch, tight and firm and yellowish brown, contented. Slender, slim, thin, and that's hard work, but who could expect otherwise?

Malcolm told me about being married to him. How we would live. The fruitful life in the tower. The delicious meals we would eat. The fine red wines. The garden. The seasons. The reading and music. The trips to cities. The trips overseas. The art galleries, the plays, the restaurants. It occurred to me that I would not stay slim in such a life. So rich, so full of event. Wonderful narratives, like a book he was giving me, inviting me to enjoy.

The thing I did not consider then is that a book is for reading. It is not a life. For the space of its turning pages you may believe you live in it, but sooner or later you must close it up. Put it back on the shelf, and look at the room you are in, a room which will say sternly to you, this is where you live, what are you making of this? The life that Malcolm had written for himself, was offering to write for me, it didn't occur to me that it wasn't my life.

My bedroom in the tower was like all the rooms, big. It had a bed with tester and curtains. In the middle was a bath in the shape of a marble boat. It sat on a carpet of pale turquoise wool ruffled like water. There was a table with a lamp, set up for writing. On it was a fat notebook, with marbled endpapers, opened at its first page, blank, and resting on it a pen with a marbled pattern to match. All this is yours, said Malcolm, and I took him to mean the book. I sat at the table and wrote in it. A woman who comes to live in a tower should keep a journal of her days. Of course I wasn't living here then but visiting, and I was hardly the maiden who ought to inhabit such a story, or rather I was a maiden but not the beautiful young one the context expected. If you squinted, looked sideways, glanced at my childish figure against the light, then, perhaps, but is that a true story? All of these things could be written down, the gold nib of the pen sliding across the silky paper of the notebook, making words with perhaps no more intent or trickery than the fine black tendrils of the quince tree gazebo against the winter white sky.

The first morning he woke me to come and see the frost. He came walking down the winding stairs into my room. There were no locked doors in this house. No hidden rooms, no passageways. No desks with secret drawers. The staircases curved openly round the walls, and you entered each room on your way to the one above. It said to you, I am a house without secrets. No doors that must not be opened. No keys indelibly staining themselves with blood.

We went out into the grey morning, through French windows on to a terrace and across meadow grass to a maze. Everything was powdered blue with frost. When you looked closely there were frail encrustations of ice, holding the cold morning light in their blue refractions. See how beautiful it is, said Malcolm. The hedges of the maze were so far only waist height, but you could still get lost, he said.

So you could get trapped, I said.

I think patience would find you a way out.

At the top of the slope was the quince tree gazebo, a dome made of arches of iron, over which were espaliered bare branches, to replicate exactly the shape of the dome. There were spaces so you could walk inside and stand in a small house of intertwined branches. In summer, said Malcolm, the quinces hang upon it, golden globes of fruit.

At the bottom of the slope was a pond, or dam I suppose, with reeds and a punt and a small wooden shack. There are birds to be watched, said Malcolm.

When we got back to the house we found a pile of long white boxes on the terrace table. These are for you, he said. Inside were nests of tissue paper and in them stems and stems of red gladioli, every kind of red, crimson, scarlet, vermilion, rose. Malcolm fetched tall glass vases and we put them in, the green thick stems under water through the glass and then the red flower buds just beginning to open. I felt surrounded by tallness and redness.

My room, Malcolm calls this bedroom. Gloria's room. The bath like a boat. The wide fireplace. The table with its marbled notebook and pen to match, inviting writing. The bed with tester and hangings in dark turquoise and indigo, the same heavy brocade at the windows. There is always a movement of air in the tower. The candle flames shimmer, the hangings stir, as the air moves through the rooms. As though the building were a creature who breathes, silently but heavily. Every now and then heaving a huge mute sigh. Draughts, I suppose they are, but not cold; the fireplaces are large and log fires burn intensely, but somewhere there is a furnace that pours hot air through the house. I lie in bed wondering if I shall wake to the faint grinding roar of machinery, to find the tester a finger's width from my face, or even not wake up at all because it will have wound its way right down and suffocated me.

But I slept, and woke to the sound of shots. Another fox. What do you do with them? I asked Malcolm. Until now, he said, I have given them to Anne the gardener, she buries them under the trees she plants. And last summer we had some fine vegetables grown over dead fox. But now—and Malcolm pulled the fox's brush between his fingers so it sleeked down and then sprang out—now I am going to have them made into a fur coat. It will match your hair, he said.

For that is the colour of my hair. Reddish, russet, foxy coloured. By nature once, these days less so.

So, will I walk through the maze spangled blue with frost like a large dainty upright fox? In the borrowed pelts of a dead animal? Perhaps I will.

After breakfast Malcolm played the harpsichord, such gentle intricate music. You listen entranced to its melodic entwinings and interleavings, it belongs to a world that is safe and ordered. Anne the gardener brought in wood and stacked it by the hearth. I sat and read. Malcolm went out again, in boots and coat and taking a gun. I didn't go. I sat and read. I sat and looked at the room.

By the staircase was a big wooden sea chest, old, worn, polished. It had brass clasps and a lock with a key. After a little while I got up and turned the key, but the chest had not been locked, I had to turn it again. Inside were folded pieces of fabric, smelling of peppermint. Ikat, and batik, brocades, embroidery. Most of them were old, some ancient, most had had another existence. I sat on the edge of the chest and lifted them out, unfolding them a little to look at them.

Malcolm came back and I started, so engrossed was I in the chest's contents, and nearly fell in. I remembered the story of the bride who disappears on her wedding day and is found decades later, a skeleton in a marriage dress, in a great chest. But Malcolm is here to save me. Unless it was the husband who shut her in. But Malcolm is not my husband yet, and he was saying with delight, Ah, you have found my treasure.

He shook out several pieces and held them up. It is a pity not to display them, he said, looking vaguely round. Perhaps, one day . . . though they are fragile.

He draped a piece of gossamer silk ikat against me. They are not for wearing, really, he said, not any more, but please, look at them sometimes. They need looking at. All beautiful things need looking at.

I did marry Malcolm. You may wonder why. Out of a desire to be married, you might think. He did not actually speak of love, but of the delights of marriage. Perhaps because I had been for many years a schoolteacher, and for my girls their time at school is such an interim. It is a stage where they alight, birds with beautiful bejewelled feathers, preen briefly and then fly off to their real lives. I saw the chance for a life of my own, not of other people's interims.

So, I married him. He chose a date in the spring. The ceremony was in the gazebo, which was covered in fresh green leaves and the starry flowers of the quince blossom. I wore a dress of greenish white satin—white because I was still a virgin, but greenish as well, to signify time—like a lily it sheathed my body and at wrists and neck unfolded in bias-cut furls edged with pale green piping. A graceful dress that followed the languid movements of my body. I carried a posy of lily of the valley with a wreath of it in my hair, and walked across the meadow thick with daffodils and bluebells, to the piping music of a recorder. Afterwards we spent the afternoon feasting at the long table; Malcolm and I sat together and watched and listened as people drank toasts and laughed and talked. The food was prepared by Gareth, the husband of Anne the gardener, who is a painter but sometimes cooks for Malcolm and cleans the house. He is not a very good painter, Malcolm says, but he can spend nearly all his time at it which makes him happy. A trio played harpsichord and various recorders and viola da gamba, the lovely intricate slightly melancholic music which is the leitmotif of this house, and is in music what the delicate complicated espaliering of the quince trees is in gardens and my lily-sheath with ruffles at neck and wrist is in dresses.

At twilight Anne drove the guests back to town in the bus Malcolm had hired and we went up to my room where the fire was burning and champagne sat in a bucket, beside a large book covered in fine-grained red morocco. The candle flames shimmered in the warm draughts of air. Malcolm poured some wine into flutes and said, now that we are married I will tell you what I write.

What he writes is pornography. One volume a year. Produced on his printing press in the basement, illustrated with etchings, or woodcuts. Limited editions of a hundred, selling for five thousand dollars each, more if he hand-washes them with watercolour. A lot of money.

What kind of pornography?

It varies, he says. Any kind, really.

Children?

Of course.

But that's pedophilia, it's disgusting.

No. It's graceful and delicate, small pretty creatures. Remember, they're not people, they're not photographs, they're drawings. No one is harmed by them.

The eyes that look at them are.

He shrugged.

And you, making them.

Do I seem damaged?

What else? I asked. Homosexuality?

He nodded.

Bestiality?

Yes. And harems. Orgies. Lesbians. Nubile schoolgirls. And the intercourse of beautiful ardent lovers.

I knew what he was talking about. The antique style of pornography. For rich men, whose wealth and honourable standing in the community was presumed to protect them from corruption. Not the vulgar cheap effects of television and movies. They use real people, said Malcolm, that is where corruption comes in, they are degrading their bodies for our delectation. But me, I am drawing lines on a page. No one is endangered.

He took up the red morocco book. It had nothing on the cover but the number ten tooled in gold. I opened it. It smelled of ink and rich paper. The pages were creamy and thick, the ink had that satisfying faint unevenness of hand printing. It was in the Japanese style, with woodblocks of lovers, entirely explicit. Had I been as ignorant as I was virginal, it would have been handy. As it was I had not quite considered that people could make love sitting up like that, opening themselves like flowers to one another's gazes and fingers, looking into one another's eyes as much as at their vigorous sexual parts. They were lewd, but tender and delicate as well.

My tongue felt thick in my throat and my skin was hot. So

I had married a pornographer. I suppose I might have thought that it was not too late for an annulment, that the marriage had not been consummated. I think I thought, he will know what to do. I stood up. Malcolm unzipped the long sheath of my dress. Underneath I was naked, no lines of underwear to mar its fluid lines. I stood there in my white satin shoes. Dressed I had been a flower, elegant and languid, undressed I was my dry tight pod-like self. He took my hand and led me to the bed, tucked me in under the doona, took his clothes off and was soon white and naked and just a little chubby in the bed with me.

Taking off the dress was my true deflowering. What followed was . . . it was like acid, corrosive and rough. He dipped his fingers in a bowl of scented oils and anointed himself and me but still there was the tearing and piercing and stinging. His weight. The reluctant sticky brown blood. Is this what lies in wait for all the cruel innocent cheerful girls?

Malcolm said, It is hard, the first time. It will be better. He rolled over and went to sleep. I wished I were a delicate etching in a book, in hand-set type on creamy paper for a connoisseur to read.

He was right of course. It does get better. And soon I think I shall begin to enjoy it.

I asked Malcolm if he would prefer me not to go up on the roof. If it was so dangerous. No, he said, whyever should that be? I said, your late wife, and he replied that it was hardly the roof. It was like a railway line, he said, not at all dangerous, unless you happened to lie on it when there was a train coming. Then of course it was lethal, but it was the train, not the line. The same was true for the roof; it was quite safe, it was the ground that had killed her.

I was not sure about this argument. There seemed some twist or bend in its logic, but I could not quite discern it. But then that is the thing with metaphoric language, it persuades you to see connections and parallels where there are none.

I wondered if the second Mrs Pembroke was up on the roof looking for marauding tribes. There never were any. Building a tower in this place against marauding tribes was like building a tower against ghosts, they melted through the landscape and you only saw them if they wanted you to. The beat of drums and the glint of sunlight on cuirass and helmet: they belong to the tales of other continents, other civilisations, they never translated here.

I am still Gloria Jones. When we go to Paris in the northern spring for our honeymoon, then I will be the third Mrs Pembroke.

I wondered about the first Mrs Pembroke. What she died of. Maybe she drowned in the pond. It is quite deep, and treacherous,

Anne said, be careful not to fall out of the punt. Anne and Gareth are not chatty. They speak when necessary, but they do not converse. They go about their work quietly and say things like, we need some more toilet cleaner. Or, mind the pond.

Your first wife, I said to Malcolm. How did she die?

I'm planning to have lunch with her, next week probably, he said. She's not dead, we agreed to part, it's amicable enough. Why don't you come and meet her? It's time we had a trip to Sydney.

I didn't go. I didn't care about meeting the first Mrs Pembroke; there could be time for that. I decided to stay in the tower. To go up on the roof. I sat on the crenellated parapet and looked at the bones of the garden. They were fleshing out with the spring growth. Maybe I could learn the pattern of the maze from here.

I felt but had no trouble resisting the pull of gravity, that seductive invitation to jump off, see what it's like. People are supposed to be charmed by heights such as this and allow themselves to fall; they don't want to die, they just can't resist the pull. At least, people speak of this pull, but they don't do it, they live to tell the tale.

Perhaps the second Mrs Pembroke was pushed. Not by her husband, he was elsewhere, so he said, and must have been believed. But maybe he hired a hit man. For not many thousands of dollars, I believe, you can hire somebody to kill a person for you, and Malcolm has a great deal of money.

I suppose a question is, why would he want to kill her? Why did Bluebeard kill his wives? Because that's what he did. It's a given. It's the plot. Until the lucky one, who is saved.

The even more interesting question is: why did Mrs Bluebeard feel utterly unable to resist opening the door? Don't we all think, when it comes to these stories, that we'd have made it work? So much freedom, and one tiny forbidden thing. Not important, a token in fact. So easy to obey so small a prohibition. We think, if I had been Eve I wouldn't have picked the fruit of the tree of the knowledge of good and evil, I wouldn't have given a piece to Adam. I and my progeny down the millennia would still be multiplying fruitfully in the Garden of Eden.

How crowded it would be. For there would be no death. And there of course, when you think of it, is the answer. Eve had to do what she did. She was following the script. That was the story. The fruit must be picked. The room must be unlocked, and the lady turns the key, staining it with telltale blood. The pomegranate seeds must be nibbled, and Persephone complies. The box must be opened, and Pandora obliges. Otherwise there is no narrative, it is just endless shapeless vegetable calm.

And it is in the hands of the women that the narratives lie. They are the ones who must make the stories happen. All through history, they have been depended on, and never failed.

Malcolm is away, but he forbids me nothing. There are no locked rooms whose key I am not allowed to employ. No boxes

I must not open, I am enjoined to look at everything. No fruits I must not eat. When the quinces are ripe, he will cook them for me himself, with honey and verjuice.

I am waiting for him to tell me what I must not do.

# VALIANT

He said:

It was at that time I was driving the old Valiant. A real monster. Built like a truck. And it had fins. I liked driving that car, it was an automatic, with a lot of power. In that kind of easygoing American style, solid, like a car in a gangster movie, with a bench seat in front and the driving somehow leisurely. Elizabeth didn't care for it at all, but we had another car, a newish Peugeot. She drove that. She was rude about the Valiant's colour, it was a pretty pale pink. How could you have bought a pink car, she said. I hadn't given the colour a thought, it was the driving I liked, and the price was a big consideration. At about the time I got it Julia was bridesmaid at a cousin's wedding and she had a dress of some silky satiny material, much the same colour, and apparently it was called Angel's Tears. So that's the name Elizabeth gave the car. Angel's Tears.

Julia was fond of the car, I promised I'd teach her to drive it when she turned sixteen. It seemed a good safe car for a young girl. Then of course I wouldn't have the Valiant to myself, but that was a problem for later. My other daughter Claude who's much younger had plans to be married from it. With a Barbie doll dressed in tulle on the front and a lot of ribbons the same colour to fly in the breeze. The women in my family didn't seem to be able to see beyond the car's pinkness. Whereas for me it was its performance.

I always drove the Valiant when I went to see Vikki. She lived on the other side of the city, in a townhouse in a kind of maze. I'd back the car into a carport at the side. So it wasn't too obvious. Though I didn't think there was anyone around to pay attention to it. There were thick dense hedges of some kind of conifer between the houses. They didn't have that fresh pine smell that's good in trees but the disinfectant stink of public lavatories over a sour smell as though all the neighbourhood cats pissed in them. I'd back the car in partly to avoid having to get out into that prickly smelly wall of bushes. Vikki said it was so I could make a quick getaway. I thought, From the scene of the crime? but never said it.

Vikki used to go on about the car, how she loved it. She didn't know Elizabeth called it Angel's Tears—enough to make the angels weep, Elizabeth said, but affectionately, she was glad for me to have a car I liked—Vikki called it Prince, or me Prince, I wasn't ever quite sure. I suppose it was me Prince, the car Valiant, but then I was her Prince Valiant sometimes too, a bit confused but it was that playful thing that only works in a besotted state. A cool glance, a sharp ear, and it's stuff to make you cringe.

That night, as always, Vikki didn't want me to go home. Stay, she said. Stay all night. I was in the car, I'd wound the window down to say goodbye, and she was leaning in, kissing me, her tongue teasing mine, begging me to stay.

You know I can't, I said.

Ring Elizabeth. Tell her you're not going back. Not ever again.

You know I can't. I have to tell her properly.

That's what you always say. But when? Vikki had her arms round my neck and was half in the car, pressing her sharp little breasts against the flesh of my shoulder, her hands holding my head, knotting themselves in my hair in the way of passion but also in these circumstances of anger, pulling and hurting, hurting a lot. I didn't like it.

It has to be the right moment, I said. Wriggling my shoulders, trying to get free. I can't do it on the phone, snap like that. You can't end twenty years like that.

It'd be the best way, said Vikki. Neat, clean, less painful in the end.

She made it sound like surgery.

I said: But not on the phone, out of the blue, in the middle of the night.

That's why you don't do it. You make it too hard. There's never a *right* time.

Vikki. It's late. We're tired. This isn't the moment, not for any of this.

Suddenly she flounced back out of the window, flipped herself along over the bonnet of the car and under the front wheel. I had the car in gear, ready to take off the moment she let go of me, and this gave me a fright. I put it into park, dragged on the brake, got out. Vikki was lying on the ground, staring up at me, her waist pushed under the front wheel. Her waist small, and made to look more so by the breadth of her hips, that ineluctable pear shape which was one of her charms. And the reason why she always wore dresses with big skirts. An unfashionable look, but seductive, you gazed at the sway of those skirts and remembered how you could bury yourself in the great dimpled hips and thighs underneath. She looked silly, staring up like that. I could tell that she felt silly, too, and for that reason would not give up. I was distraught. I knew we were in for another battle of wills. Angry, stupid, unwinnable. Sex should never be about winning.

Stay the night, she said. Or you'll have to drive over me.

No, I said. You know I can't.

Drive over me, then, she said. It's the best way.

And do you know, I thought, yes it is. If I get in the car and drive away, drive over her—and don't forget it was a great tank of a car and I could have put my foot down and accelerated out of there, in the quick getaway gangster act—I thought, if I put my foot down and drive away, that will solve everything. No more scenes in the night, no more promises, no more evenings spent not in my office, not writing my book. The book might even get written.

And then I thought, but I'd get caught. Tyre tracks traceable. The carport private, but nowhere safe from prying eyes. Not from a baby pink Valiant. Called Angel's Tears.

That's why I didn't do it. And of course I wouldn't have liked the blood, the mess, her death on my hands. But there and then I did want to get back in and accelerate off and have done.

I said, Don't be stupid, Vikki, please. We've both had too much whisky to play games like this.

Whisky is the drink of adultery, Vikki always said, pouring hearty doses into cut glass tumblers, with plenty of soda and ice. Sometimes dipping her breast in it and giving it to me to suck. And indeed whisky was refreshing, after all the heat and sweating. Pleasantly prickly on the tongue and then the kick of the alcohol. I'd take her bottles of something okay but not great, Teachers, Dewars, whatever was on special, whisky not normally one of my drinks. Except occasionally a single malt with a teaspoon of still water. Vikki was always trying to get me to come and have dinner with her, like a normal couple, but I ate at home with Elizabeth and the children, the evening meal being important in our house, though I drank only one glass of wine. To keep a clear head for the book, I said, but indeed it was not my head that I was concerned about on these evenings. With Vikki so much younger than me I needed to be sure I would not fail to rise to the occasion.

I got back in the car, revved the engine. Making sure it was safely in park. She stayed where she was. Both of us knew she was perfectly safe.

I got out of the car. Come *on*, Vikki, I said. This is just a waste of time. You're going to ruin our alibi. If I'm too late I'm not writing the book.

I *want* to ruin your alibi. I want to break your alibi. Break it into little tiny pieces. Annihilate it. And you'll never need it again. Never.

Vikki, I said. For god's sake. This isn't the way. I can't do it like this.

I got hold of her arm and tried to pull her out. But hadn't a hope. She turned herself into a dead weight. All that powerful pear-shape being solid flesh.

You'll ruin your . . . your . . . I couldn't think of the word. Housecoat wasn't it. Negligée, I suppose, but it wasn't a word I was happy to say. Dressing gown, Elizabeth would have said, but not of this. Your clothes, I said, though it was more unclothes. It was some flimsy pale blue thing, thin, fragile looking, with frills and lace. An item of intimate apparel, you might say, if you were a policeman, and the intimacy wasn't only with the wearer's body, which was anyway tenuous, it was what it invited from the body of her companion. Under normal circumstances.

Slowly she pulled up the frilly layers. She wasn't wearing any pants. She pulled the garment up above her waist, so I could see the wide curve of her hips and the small pale fuzz of her hair. Slowly she parted her legs, raising her knees at the same time. Looking at me with the slightly glazed eyes of lust. She didn't seem to realise that what she was offering me wasn't her pretty fanny that I loved to kiss and press my face into. It was more like a wound, red and secret, that I was obliged to see against my will, the embarrassing and disturbing act of a beggar exposing herself in return for gain. Using her sex to persuade me made it a transaction, a commercial exchange, and herself a whore, goods coldly regarded: are they worth the price?

Kiss me, she said.

I started thinking of newspaper headlines. Not so much the Distinguished Historian Caught Copulating Under Car variety, but sad and solitary ones: Woman's Scantily Clothed Body In Shallow Grave sort of thing. Those have always seemed to me heartbreaking, those images of women's bodies that were in life cosseted and offered only to the gaze of love, now exposed and prey to ugly eyes and the roughness of stones and dirt. Desired flesh turned into human meat.

I leaned down and pulled the flimsy fabric across her nakedness. A rough edge of my fingernail caught in it and snagged. Vikki, I said. I went and sat in the car, sideways, feet on the ground. I thought of the book I wasn't writing. A sentence came into my mind: *The alienation of suburbia needs to be recognised as a more or less nourishing myth, a construct of a Bohemian perception of city life* . . . Or perhaps *a construct of Bohemian angst*, giving a nice resonance between *alienation* and *angst*, though I wasn't sure whether angst could construct anything . . . My notebook and pen, which I am never without, were in my jacket in the back seat. I leaned quietly over. If Vikki noticed what I was doing she'd go mad.

You might wonder why I couldn't write the book at home, and of course I could have. But my story was the files, the books, the computer with the particular connections to the library and such. All these I could have organised to have at home. But I told Elizabeth it was better at work. She believed me. She trusted me.

I went inside the house and poured out two more whiskies, weak, with plenty of soda and ice. I said to myself, I could get done for drink driving and that would be a solution. No more night alibis.

Vikki was still lying under the wheel. The tyre looked a bit bald, I'd have to get a new one soon, more expense. It was cold, and the ground was part stubbly grass, part concrete drive strip, it must be very hard and chilly by now. I put the glass by her head and went and sat again in the driver's seat. It was ten past twelve. I took sips of the whisky. The drink of adultery.

Of the desperate, more like. Mine was nearly gone when I heard the rustle of her movement. Hers was untouched, and she threw it in my face. All down my shirt and jumper.

You're such a shit, she said, and went inside.

I drove home. Elizabeth's bedside light was on, she always left it on for me, so I wouldn't have to go to bed in the dark. I took off my shirt and jumper and left them in the car. That would stink of alcohol now. The night air was freezing on my whisky wet skin. I found myself humming *He who would valiant be* . . . it's a hymn, I believe. I know it's a hymn. *To be a pilgrim*. When I say humming, I mean in my head. Cynically. Savagely even. I wished Vikki wouldn't make things so sordid. *He who would valiant be* . . . I crept in and sluiced myself down as best I could, keeping silent about it. She'd thrown the whisky, rather than poured it over the top of my head, so my hair hadn't copped too much. What there is of it, hair.

Elizabeth murmured when I got into bed, but hardly stirred. I was slow going to sleep. The night had been so stupid; the marvellous part, the sex, the love talk, the lovely secret conversation, so blithe somehow, sunny, like a stream chattering along and us in an Adam and Eve innocence, inventing sex for the first time, all so ruined. So soured. And I kept thinking about where I was in the book, and where I might have been.

I was in a first deep sleep when the phone rang. Three am. Vikki. Her voice slurred. I've had more whisky and a bottle of pills, she said.

Elizabeth had jumped awake, in the terror of three-am phone calls. Her mother, sisters . . . inventories of disaster.

Vikki, I said.

Elizabeth groaned. She's not committing suicide again?

Hang up the phone, I said, and dial triple O. Now. Go on. I can't come. Not tonight. I tell you what, hang up and *I'll* dial triple O. No, no, Vikki, this can't go on. Hang up the phone. Hang up the phone.

She did hang up after a while, and I dialled the ambulance. Elizabeth turned to me and we lay with our arms around one another. Thank goodness, she said. You've run around after that silly girl long enough. She ought to get rid of that hopeless boyfriend, he's no good to her.

You're right, I said.

And it's not as though she's your student any more. There's a limit to responsibility.

Yes, I said, and we went to sleep, the familiar entwined long-loving sleep of old married couples.

I rang the hospital next day but Vikki had been sent home. You bastard, she said. She was okay. They hadn't needed to pump her stomach out this time, she hadn't actually taken a great many pills, she was too drunk, and she'd managed to vomit up a lot of the whisky.

I am a bastard, I said. And an old married man. I can't stop, I said. Being married.

That wasn't the end of it, but it was the beginning of the

end. I started working on the book at home. Drank red wine with Elizabeth at dinner. Good bottles, sometimes, sometimes only okay, but fine to drink.

So there you have it. Not an edifying story. All too common. The married man and the young woman. She believes he will leave his wife for her. So does he. But he doesn't. He is that kind of bastard. He deceives himself as well as the girl, but in the end he is not taken in as the girl is. There's another narrative, in which the man does leave his wife, and in that he's another kind of bastard. Neither is an attractive tale, but there would be no narrative if they were. Just a comfortable married couple drinking wine. The bastard stories are stories women like to tell. But this one's mine, so I am telling it. Not really to anyone. It's an insomnia narrative shaped and polished while Elizabeth lies snoring gently beside me. I wouldn't hurt her by writing it down. But I work on it, quite often, when I can't sleep. Add the details, the stinking conifers, the breast dipped in whisky, the bare tyre. Her sex like a wound. Little touches.

## THE WHITE PEACOCK

He is a nice man. He asks me to do things with him. I say no. Every time. He doesn't ask all that often, he's quite timid, but he is also dogged. As though he has dares with himself, and must go through with them. I decline with politeness and almost excessive regret. I'm so sorry, Vaughan, I can't . . . I'm going . . . they are coming . . . I've promised . . . I said I would . . . It is probably this excessive politeness that allows him to go on asking me.

There are never many women in the bar. The women in this town are mostly mothers and at this after-work hour are at home with the tea and the children. There are some older women who are free, mostly the young leave. I have reversed this process, having come. I'm the schoolteacher. I have my own house beside the school, rather larger in fact than the school, and after one or perhaps two glasses of wine I will go home to it and light the fire and make a meal. Dan who runs the pub opens bottles of red wine for me though normally he wouldn't sell it by the glass. The men drink beer. They stand at the bar and hitch their bellies. I sit at a table by the fire and sometimes they pause and talk to me. They don't sit down, only the card players sit down.

Sometimes lean men in worn tight jeans come into the pub. They prop booted feet on the bar rail and push their Akubras to the backs of their heads. Brad and Rod and Marvin and Joe. From the farms and the sawmill. Nino and Hughie from the garage on the main road. Gerhardt from the bakery. He wears a baseball cap. The kids at school wear similar caps but with big flaps round their necks to save them from the sharp high-country sun. I lean on the bar for a moment and have a word. Some of the men have children in the school. Some are just passing through.

I sit with the glass of red by the fire and stare into it. The fire is a friend. A present companion, silent but always fascinating. You can gaze into the fire and think and not feel lonely. When the men address their remarks to me it can feel like an interruption. Today the topic is the snow, a very good thing, it will melt and gently soak the poor droughty ground. I think they are shy, not that it shows among themselves but they do not believe they have anything to say to me. They know my name is Jess but don't call me by it.

Vaughan is not tall or lean, he's stocky. His bottom is too

big, it's plump, not hard. The men with their huge beer bellies tight and taut as drums—I imagine walking along and playing them, different notes booming out as I beat my hands against them—these men have neat buttocks, their jeans sit under their stomachs and fit firmly around their bottoms, whereas Vaughan is rather full in the hips, though his belly is flat enough, and his jeans bunch around his middle. Have I come here to this forsaken country on the cold rind of the world to look at men's bums? When I was married to one I did not pay so much attention; it was a pleasant part of a body that I loved and lusted after. When a man says he does not care in that way for you any more, the marriage is over though we can still be friends, why not, good friends as we have been lovers and partners over the years, you have to put away loving and lusting and get on with another life and coming here to this cold rind of the world seemed a good idea. You can look at men's bums or stare into the fire and drink your glass of red which is halfway decent and remember the article in today's paper which said people, especially women, who drink wine, a lot of wine, five or six bottles a week, think better, their brains work better. And come to think of it I suppose I think quite well; I certainly do a lot of it.

Vaughan has shining clean brown hair that flops around his head in a messy silky fashion and rosy cheeks in a plump soft face. His skin is very pale brown and then there are these two patches of flaming red on his cheeks. He speaks gently and looks as though his clothes are ironed. He lives with his parents and works on the farm. I suppose his mother irons his clothes for him. He looks very young, and even allowing for the fact that he's probably not as young as he looks, he's not very old, not rugged and weather-beaten like the other men, even the younger ones. Certainly a good bit younger than me.

He is a nice man, Vaughan. Who wants to be nice? In my day the mothers of girls wanted them to be nice but the daughters didn't. I think the mothers of sons probably didn't care about their boys being nice. Mothers of daughters say, he seems a nice boy, and the daughters don't think that's a good thing either, who wants a nice boy, and anyway what would mothers know. The men with the big bellies, the lean rugged cowboys (sheepboys?) are probably very nice men too, but somehow it isn't how you think of them, and with Vaughan it is.

That day Vaughan sat down at my table. He said, A fire is like the sea. You can look and look at it and never get tired.

I thought this was a good thing to say. I smiled. He said, Jess? I am going to the sea. Would you like to come? On Saturday.

Oh Vaughan, that's a nice idea. Except, I'm sorry, I've got . . .

There's a peacock garden.

A peacock garden?

A garden with peacocks.

Peacocks . . . the sea . . .

I found I had said yes.

I'll pick you up at eight o'clock. Get a good start. He finished his beer, waved to the blokes at the bar and left. I wished I hadn't said yes. Down the mountain in his dusty old ute. What if it didn't have good brakes? I'd been going to stay home on Saturday and sit in front of the fire and read. Lorna gave me Patrick White's *Twyborn Affair* when I told her I was coming here. The Monaro plateau, she said, it's so important in that book, you have to read it. Well, Patrick White's not really my thing, we had to study some awful boring full-of-incomprehensible-abstract-meaning novel of his in one of my courses and I swore off him forever. But being here, I thought I should. One day. This Saturday. Now it will have to be another one day.

When he came it wasn't the old ute but a shiny four-wheel drive. The parents', he said, they lent it to me so we could be comfortable.

Did your mother also inquire whether I am a nice girl, I wondered, but then I am hardly a girl, having wasted eight years of my life on a marriage which failed. Not me, not Sam, it wasn't us that failed, it was the marriage. Like a baby that didn't thrive, grew sickly, died. But then we would have blamed ourselves. Whereas a marriage that fails, it's somehow its fault. So Sam would have it. The car was white and cosy with leather seats and good heating. I hate four-wheel drives but I have to confess it was fun sitting high up looking at the world. I thought, this isn't a date, this is going to the sea with a nice man. I said, I was planning to stay at home and read Patrick White.

I don't know why I said it. To put him off perhaps. Telling him you've got a clever one here. Making myself a formidable woman, a terrifying woman. Not a woman to take on dates. Provided he knew who Patrick White was, of course, he might think he's the latest thriller writer. In which case I would already have read the book, I can never resist thrillers.

*The Twyborn Affair*? Haven't you read it yet, he said. You must, living here.

You've read it then?

I reckon. It was one of our family farms he came to, over the way a bit, I could show you some time. It's still a family story. The blooding of young Patrick. And of course, you have to ask, did he do those things?

Did you like it?

Yeah. Not so much as *Riders in the Chariot*. Or *The Vivisector*. But I liked it. He knows how to make you feel the Monaro.

The cold rind of the world . . .

Where the wind wuthers, said Vaughan.

There was a lot of snow still, heaped by the side of the road, lying in striations across the bare paddocks, caught in the serrated tussock, and when we started the descent from the plateau, where there were sparse forests of trees, the ground between them was covered with a thick blanketing fall. It's like Germany, said Vaughan. I know the trees are different but the way the snow piles on the ground, and drifts over the bushes, and powders the branches. And you can see how quiet it is.

Waiting for a fairytale to happen. Grimm, or someone. A wicked stepmother.

Hansel and Gretel and the birds pecking up the bread.

He pressed a button and a CD started playing. Elton John. That line, living like lovers, it gets to me, I don't know why. I didn't say much as the car wound down the mountain, just listened to Elton.

We crossed the river, going into Merimbula. It's a very wide river, I said. He explained that ships used to come right up, big ships, loading and unloading; the granite for the Harbour Bridge pylons came from the Merimbula quarries, he said. I imagined great blocks of stone loaded on to ships, sailing up the coast to Sydney.

We had coffee by the water at Merimbula and looked at the big game-fishing cruisers with their towering wheelhouses and massive rods, the chairs fitted with harnesses and fastened to the deck. And the whale boats tied up at the wharf. The whale boats being whale watching boats, not whale hunting any more.

We got to Eden by lunchtime and bought fish and chips at the wharf and drove up to the beach and ate them at a table on the edge of the sand. Vaughan had bought a bottle of red wine and long-stemmed glasses. I hope you don't mind red wine with fish, he said. I think it's okay with fish and chips. Oysters, now . . . He shook his head. Out in the bay a pod of dolphins swam up and down, cleaving through the water, not showily jumping up and curving down in their playful disporting way, but more serious, fishing. Vaughan was right, you can stare at the sea and never grow tired, especially when there are dolphins threading through it.

The sun shone down on us, the air was cool but balmy, the red wine was beneficent, especially as I was getting more than my fair share, since Vaughan was driving. I told him about wine drinking improving thinking. He pointed out Ben Boyd's tower, which Boyd meant for a lighthouse but was never allowed to, because he wanted to have it working only when he wanted to, and lighthouses have to be all the time or not at all. He talked about the killer whales who herded the other whales into the bay so the whalers could kill them. Like dogs with sheep, he said. Most of the time we just sat, watching the birds, the maimed seagulls, the brown speckled ducks that looked like eagles when they flew, the water that stretched smooth between the arms of the bay like a piece of taut blue silk. I said that and he laughed. I know it's a cliché, I said, but sometimes clichés are just right.

After lunch we walked through the cemetery which was a kind of paddock sloping gently away from the sea and all its headstones facing towards the water, tall and upright and as if staring out at it. I suppose, I said, they are all sailors, gazing out at the sea they spent their lives on. Mariners at rest, though still paying attention. But they were mostly the town's fathers, and mothers, the mothers often dead young and the children too. One small grave was enclosed by a fence of elaborate ironwork like a cot for the child who slept there. Some of the headstones were too old and worn to read, just the occasional stroke of a letter remaining. I like cemeteries, they are melancholy places but full of lives. The fathers, the mothers, the children, the families, deaths in childbirth, in accidents, in safe old ages, they are all stories, some of them sad, some tragic: that is the human condition. And the human connection, clearer in death. It's comforting that it's all been done before. I think of never having a baby, but at least I would not have to suffer from its dying.

We pottered about, sometimes calling to one another to come look at some poignant thing, some piece of bad poetry about the afterlife, some lengthy tender message, some pompous worldly claim. I remembered a strange movie I'd seen, very late at night and years ago, the kind that was made to be second rate, to accompany the main picture, about a man who somehow went back in time and fell in love with a woman, a doomed love since he had to return to his own time, and over the sad kisses of their parting she promised that when she died she'd have her headstone cut very deep, so the words would last, and the final scene is him back in his own present and going to the cemetery and finding her tombstone among all the other half-obliterated ones, and tracing the deeply carved letters with his fingers. So silly really, and hopelessly romantic; some impossible notion of love beyond the grave, love there in those deeply etched letters, and yet I remember it, and what does that say? That I want to believe in eternal love, love as permanent as words deep in stone? I gazed at the worn stones in this graveyard with their obliterated words and it seemed particularly sad that the stone remained but the message that was its reason for being was entirely lost. Time stealing what was meant to defeat it.

A wind came in from the sea, ruffling its silk, worrying its fishy grey surface into scurrying waves, fanning Vaughan's rosy cheeks brighter red. His jeans were still baggy but you couldn't see his bottom under a heavy parka.

We got into the car and made our way to the peacock garden which turned out not to be public but the property of some friends of his who were away; he called in from time to time, to cast an eye, he said. There was a long drive from a locked gate through rich forest and the slow falling notes of bellbirds, then a grand house with shuttered windows and dry stone walls forming terraces covered with leaf litter, dropping down to a dam. The peacocks strutted the mulchy slopes of the terraces and cried their terrible cries like abandoned children. I don't think I could live with peacocks, there is too much pain in their voices; I know it isn't so for them but I couldn't bear such anguished meaningless cries. Vaughan prowled round the house and I sat quietly on an iron bench. After a while he came and stood behind me and then the peacocks began to dance. Three magnificent males and a small brown peahen. The males spread their tails and danced, and I marvelled that such gorgeous heavy swathes of feathers could be supported on such small bird bodies. They arched and stepped and fluttered their tails and the small brown peahen took no notice. What *peacocks*, I murmured, so extravagant, so spectacular. So vain. And the peahen such a small dull thing.

Yes, said Vaughan, but who has the power? Look how she ignores them.

Just then a bird came from a small copse, its tail folded behind it like a fan, drooping towards the ground but held proudly out of the dirt. At a little distance it unfurled its tail and began to strut too, rattling its feathers in a shimmying dance. It was pure white and I breathed a sigh, it was so astonishingly beautiful. So much more beautiful than the brilliant blue birds, who now seemed gaudy, vulgar, over-painted. This white was so pure, so dazzling, so angelic. White was magic, white was desire.

The peacocks danced, their tales shimmered, the peahen took no notice. Occasionally one moved towards her and nonchalantly she stepped away. Suddenly, as one approached, she turned her bottom to him and he sprang upon her, shimmered violently several times, and the act was done. They all folded their tails and strolled off, making small pecks at the leaf litter.

All that display, said Vaughan, for one little dull brown bird. And she chooses. They're gorgeous but she chooses.

I'd have chosen the white one, I said. He's by far the most beautiful.

She never will. However beautiful he is, however well he dances, she will never choose him. He is not right. It's the shimmer of the blue, that's what turns her on. He might as well be white washing on a line. He's not sexy.

You mean, no peahen will ever have him?

No. He's a sport. An albino. Peacock is blue. You know that. If I say peacock you think blue, these particular rich cobalts, turquoises, indigos. That's what a peahen needs to see. The white bird cannot breed, his kind will die out. Until another sport appears.

Nature is very cruel.

Of course. You know that.

And of course I do. I thought of the cemetery. Of the young women who die in childbirth. Of the babies who survive for days or months or maybe a year, and then are called to a better place, or so their parents want to think and write it on their tombstones to help them believe it. God wanted another angel, the stones say. The child was too good for this sinful world.

Yes, I said, I do know that. But somehow I have to keep realising it.

Do you think, I said, that the white peacock knows he will never make it?

I wonder, said Vaughan. They're not supposed to be very clever birds. Maybe he lives in hope.

Being beautiful.

There was a peacock feather with its single glittering bronze and indigo eye lying on the leaf litter. Vaughan picked it up and bowing slightly presented it to me. I was reluctant. Peacock feathers are bad luck, I said.

Are they? In China they bestow honour. They indicate the emperor's regard.

Do they? You're making that up . . .

Would I do that? And think of the land of the peacock throne. Why would they be bad luck rather than honour, when they're so gorgeous?

He opened the door of the four-wheel drive for me and waited while I climbed in. He put on a CD of Bach, that's what he said it was. Bach! I thought I should have brought my own. Savage Garden. Silverchair. But it was okay, pretty, really, tumbling somersaulting notes with a very pure energy to them. It was dark twilight, with snow clouds bunching. The car filled with the Bach notes singing, and Vaughan drove us up the mountain.

## A GROVE OF OLIVES

Once I had to bury a cat. She was a beautiful cat, lithe of limb, delicate, a great leaper. Slender and brown, a long-legged, silky-furred Burmese. She was called Dido, for reasons important at the time. When my neighbour knocked on the door and said, There is a cat in the middle of the road, it looks like yours, I said, Oh no, I don't think it would be. Because she was young and quick and clever and would not get run over. But it was her. I still can't understand how it could have happened. Mine was a quiet street, going nowhere, the traffic was always local, and not fast. I'd had no fears of her wandering the neighbourhood, crossing the road. I wondered if it was somehow deliberate, a wanton act of destruction.

I picked her up. She was already stiff, her fur dull, all the fluid movement gone out of her. She was whole, unmarked, there was no evidence of the blow that killed her. I laid her on the table on the terrace and sat beside her and mourned. There was a place down the backyard for a grave, where the soil was friable and leaf-littered. Tree roots made digging the hole hard, but with a mattock it was soon done. I couldn't bear the thought of earth clogging her fur, sifting into her ears and nostrils; it seemed too cruel, too careless, to bury her without a shroud. She was a cat, but I understood why people need to perform certain acts of burial. In the linen press I found an old sheet of fine linen that had worn through and had a great split in it. I tore off a whole bit and wrapped her in that, and laid her in the earth. A loved creature cannot be tossed away like rubbish. When I was at school I played Antigone, a sister who risks her ruler's displeasure and indeed incurs death at his hands, because she cannot bear not to bury her brother, though the king considers him disgraced and has forbidden it. Her punishment is to be buried alive, and still she believes she must perform her sacred duties.

So I laid her in the earth, and wept, and spoke the words of Hamlet's mother over Ophelia's grave: *and from her fair and unpolluted flesh May violets spring*. I did not think them in any way too grand for my Dido. And I knew violets would grow there, because they were all about, and I pulled some runners across and tucked them into the newly dug soil. I put a small rock to mark the place. Not a cross, she wasn't a Christian cat, her rites were not of that church. The violets spread, vegetation encroached, I remembered her grave, and never dug there.

I say these things to make it clear that I am a person who takes burial of the dead seriously. So it will be understood that some years later when I found myself with a human body it was by no means easy to work out how to dispose of it. I should say we, I was not alone in my dilemma. Well, to an extent I was, since my companion in the crime (no, not murder, oh no, I deny there was any murder involved) did not have my deep desire for dignity in the matter. He'd have found a pit and chucked it in, dug a shallow grave and raked it over, put it in a skip, even. We argued about that. I pointed out that ground dug over like that bears the evidence for years. How do you know? he asked. I told him I had read an article about shallow graves, how they remain as evidence for a long time (years I think it is); it is clear that the ground has been disturbed and something has been buried. He was prepared to listen to this argument, since he was keen not to get caught disposing of a body, which of course is a crime.

I suppose I should say how this came about.

We had not long come to live in a house in the hinterland, a long way and another life from the suburban street where Dido was killed, a handsome old Queenslander that had seen better days, its paint worn away to bare boards, and those much attacked by white ants. It was up on stilts, with wide verandas and a lot of fretwork. From its back veranda you could see the distant misty towers of Surfers Paradise, forlorn was always the word that came to my mind. We never went there, except to a supermarket on the outskirts, and to one of the remoter beaches to swim. It seemed a devious sort of place; even the beaches had a habit of disappearing. In Surfers I always thought that life was elsewhere; in the hinterland you could believe it was quite nearby. The landscape was green, there was a creek. We had some goats, and chooks, vegetables, mango trees. Not self-sufficient, not at all. We worked from home, often congratulating ourselves on our luck at being members of the generation that could use computers to earn a living far from a workplace. Not a rich living, we weren't interested in working the hours necessary for that, but comfortable enough with the aid of our farmlet. I was teaching myself to make goat cheese, and was pleased with my success. We ate it very fresh, the way I like it, aged goat cheese not being a favourite of mine. In the mornings I sat on the veranda drinking coffee and idly thinking, staring at those towers that distance robbed of their usual shabbiness. Thinking: I did a lot of it. Not I suppose like a philosopher, with an orderly set of useful conclusions, but for the pleasure of it.

Until his brother found us. Found us out, perhaps I should say. Turned up with a backpack and settled in for a nice long visit. So he said. Muttering sideways remarks about the only family left to take him in. Raymond hated his brother. I could see why. So did I, after a short acquaintance. But that's not my story, I don't want to waste my brain on hatred. That last night, he'd drunk nearly our week's supply of wine in just a few hours and was slurring and aggressive. With a resentment age-old and cultivated, revealing depths and refinements that made you feel sick. He grabbed Raymond and was trying to put his hands round his neck when Raymond shoved him hard away from him. He reeled back, fell against the railings, the white-anted railings, which broke and sent him tumbling to the ground.

He might have been all right, the drunk sometimes fall safely, had it not been for one of several large terracotta pots placed just where he fell. The pot broke, and the pieces gashed and smashed his head in. There was a lot of blood. He died straightaway.

Tell me we should have called the police. Raymond wouldn't, didn't. By the time he might have changed his mind, and I don't know that he did, it was too late. To me it was so clearly an accident, a drunken fall off a dodgy balcony, but Raymond said no, the police would see more sinister meanings, and I suppose he knew things I didn't. He said, Best just get rid of the body.

We rolled him in an old tarpaulin and put him under the house, that famous under-the-house of old Queenslanders, so useful for so much detritus. In the morning we would decide what to do with him.

Raymond had various ideas. Drop him from a road bridge on to the railway line. Put him on the highway, just round a sharp bend, where trucks pass. I said he'd be found immediately and it would be clear that he had been dead much longer than the accident allowed. Do you reckon, said Raymond, doubtfully. I said I was sure, and I was, fairly. Take him up to Springbrook and push him over a cliff. Find a mineshaft and throw him in.

I'm as fond as the next person of reading and watching crime dramas; I asked myself what they did, what foolproof means they had of getting rid of bodies. Trouble was that the whole point of these narratives was that there were no foolproof methods, people always got caught.

If you go up to the top of one of those devious towers, not that high, thirteenth or fourteenth floor, to have a drink, or maybe a meal, to visit somebody staying in a hotel, if you look west, not east to the sea, you can look out at the ground spread away all around you, and what you see is the canals. People like us who live in the hinterland despise the people who live on the canals. Blond-dyed women in cat's-eye sunglasses with enamelled make-up and lashings of gold jewellery, dressed in designer clothes and high-heeled sandals that turn their pudgy ankles. Dwelling in their tacky McMansions with water frontages, clumsy little jetties and even imported sandy beaches, edged by the sullen canal waters. Nearly all of these man-made canals are wrongly designed, without sufficient tidal flow to keep them clean, flush them out. The water sits brownish and filmed, near enough to stagnant, and the blue sky cannot find its reflection there. The first time I saw this, when we were staying in a hotel, before we'd found our house, I looked down and remembered all the things I'd heard about canals. Bodies on towpaths. Stinking industrial sludge. Shopping trolleys half immersed. Rapes, murders. Bodies surfacing years later. Rubbish floating. Canals in these circumstances are never pretty, and looking down at these terrifying houses shouldering at one another and the dark water lying around them, I thought, evil resides here.

Raymond said, drinking coffee on the veranda, pretending to take no notice of the body tucked away underneath us: We will put him in a canal.

Yes?

We'll weigh him down naturally somehow so he doesn't surface. When he does it'll look as though he fell in, hit his head and drowned.

No it won't, I said. He won't have any water in his lungs.

Well, hit his head and died and fell into the canal.

We can't do that, I said. We can't do that with a dead body. We have to treat it with respect and dignity.

I remembered my cat, whom I'd wrapped in a fine linen sheet and buried beneath violets.

Raymond was shaking his head. Don't you see, he said, if we bury it properly people will know we have done so, they'll think we killed him. To make it look like an accident we can't bury him respectfully.

I could see the logic of this. It is one of my problems, that I can see the logic of other people's arguments.

Leave him where he is.

We'd soon start noticing him.

Of course I hadn't meant that, really. I was expressing my despair at finding a solution.

Anyway, said Raymond, he doesn't deserve a proper burial.

You can't say that, I said. In death everybody deserves respect.

He wasn't a nice person. Throwing him to the sharks would be too good for him.

It's not him, it's us. It's us behaving well. That's what matters.

We got a boat and puttered along the canals. The big ugly houses were all so close together there was no room for gardens, just terraces and swimming pools and this grungy water. The houses were too horrible to look at and the water wasn't attractive either.

What would you put in his pockets? I asked.

Beer bottles?

Oh, very Kenneth Slessor.

I suppose that could be dangerous, said Raymond. A literary reference. It's just that it's appropriate, given his enthusiasm for emptying them.

What about a telescope? He was walking out on a jetty to look at the stars—perve on the girls in hotel bedrooms—tripped, hit his head, died, fell in.

Telescope? Clever. But we don't have one. If we bought one it could be traced. And expensive.

Binoculars?

Ditto.

You're overlooking the main problem, I said. That very thing—the overlooking. Every window you can see, every house along the banks, they can all see us chucking our body in the water.

We looked around. I imagined couples in darkened hotel rooms, making love, gazing out at the view.

The trouble is, I said, your genuine industrial canal, of film and literature, is a dark and secret place. It slinks along its hidden path.

Okay, he said. We give up on canals.

I suppose I got my way in the end. Decent burial. Some way from the house, down the slope, we dug over the soil in quite a large area. In one part we made a deepish hole. In the night we rolled brother down in his tarpaulin, stopped beside the hole.

The tarp'll make it take a long time to rot, said Raymond.

So I got a sheet, a perfectly good one, I didn't have any ripped ones at that moment, but it was polyester and I hate polyester, never use it, and was glad to see the back of it. We wrapped him in that, holding our breath, tipped him in the hole. Covered it over. It did indeed look dug up, but not just the grave, the whole bed. We planted nine olive trees. Olive trees mean continuity, long years of peace, they take seven years to come into production so if your enemy destroys them you are without livelihood for all that time. Raymond and I may go, die or depart, but the olive trees will remain. No one need dig them up to harvest them. I expect olives historically grew in soil with corpses in it. You can sit on the veranda and watch the silver turning of their leaves in the mild winds, and think of fruitfulness and order. And unpleasant brother buried beneath. The most use that bloke's ever been in his life, said Raymond.

# AT THE END OF NO LINE

When Marcus rang her up on her mobile phone he always asked, Where are you? First of all he said, Hello, Marcus here, and then, How are you, to which Nissa would reply, I am well, oh yes, I am well, with a lilt in her voice because when he was on the phone she was well indeed. Then he would say, in his tender curious voice, Where are you?

Do you notice you always say that? she said.

It's because it's a mobile phone, he replied. I want to picture you, where you are. If you had the phone to your home I would know how to imagine you, in your sitting room in the old leather chair. Warming your feet on the fender. Gazing out the window.

Seeing the world all wavery and watery, through the panes of old glass.

Nissa lived a little way outside the town in an old cottage

with thick stone walls, with barely electricity and certainly no telephone. Perhaps if she decided to buy it she would have the telephone put on.

Where are you? asked Marcus.

I'm sitting on a spindly wooden seat at the bottom of the garden, looking at the nice juicy ground I've been digging, thinking about vegetables to plant in the spring.

You're going to grow vegies?

Of course.

Where are you?

I'm walking up the little hill behind the house. The knob. Where the slopes look like mangy but noble lions.

It must be cold.

Oh yes. And the air smells of frost.

What does frost smell like?

Cold. Very pure. Mineral. Not like things growing. Or the sea air full of salt and buffeting.

Her replies are becoming artful, even poetic, designed to entrance him.

Where are you?

I am sitting by my fire with a book, reading the love sonnets of Elizabeth Barrett Browning, drinking red wine, thinking . . .

Of me?

Who else?

Oh Nissa.

Where are you?

I am curled up under my doona, quite naked, with only my breasts for company. Like little round warm birds.

Where are you?

In the main street. Crossing by the stone bridge. A woman in search of goat cheese.

Ah, I wish I had known. We could have had a cup of coffee.

She cannot phone him at work in case his wife is there. They run the business together, working from home, and are rarely apart. He rings Nissa on his way to the bank or the post office or errands like that, even the shopping he and his wife do together. Telephoning is hard, meeting harder.

Where are you?

Picking nuts. I've found a copse of hazelnuts at the bottom of the paddock, shiny brown, with little leafy caps. Such bounty.

I thought you'd be at the computer.

Oh, a few things to do first.

The computer was how it had all started. First they'd met at a party. Everybody in town knew that Nissa had sold her restaurant and come to live in the old cottage. Arguably the best restaurant in the country, people said wisely to one another. And now she is living here. They were keen to meet her. So there were parties, dinners, drinks, log fires, questions.

What brings you to our little town, so far from home? asked the mayor.

Home, said Nissa. Maybe I'm trying to find out where that is.

The mayor laughed. Everybody was a bit frightened of Nissa. She had such standards. She was so pure, so clear. They thought they were very brave, inviting her to eat their food. Though Jane had read in a magazine that she liked things to be plain and homely. But very good, of course. The thing is, to be honest, said Jane. That's what she likes. Authenticity. Jane lived in a house her husband's family had built in 1869.

Marcus did not ask her why she'd come. He said, Have you seen the Rosalie Gascoigne in the gallery?

Gascoigne is why I came, said Nissa. I saw that exhibition she had in Sydney last year and fell in love with her. I got one of the Monaro grasses, of course not as big as the piece you have here. But just as mysteriously heart-stoppingly beautiful. So I thought, that is where to live. Among the yellow grasslands.

Ah, then you know about the landscape.

Gascoigne. And Patrick White, when I first read him I was so moved by those accounts in *The Twyborn Affair*. Cleansing, scouring. A kind of ritual to be moved through. I'm sure you know all that.

Marcus did, in fact, though other people at the table didn't, and felt nervous. They were not sure they spoke her language.

Marcus wondered if she were testing them, to see what they knew about the place they lived in turned into art.

Do I know the Gascoigne in the gallery? asked Kellie, Marcus's wife.

You know it. That very wide picture, on the end wall, slivers of wood, yellow, a whole lot of fragments, actually bits of soft drink cases, making the landscape.

Oh, that, said Kellie.

You want to go out Nimmitabel way, see what the landscape can really do, said the mayor.

Oh yes, I long for that, said Nissa.

And keep right on going, down Brown Mountain to the coast, said a man called Ed.

That's where you're wrong, said the mayor. It's not just somewhere to be got through on the way to elsewhere.

It's barren, it's bleak, it gives me the willies.

You need to learn to see it.

I hear you're writing a book, said Belinda. Is it a recipe book?

Nissa hung her head. I sometimes think that the only way I'm at all a real writer is being superstitious of talking about it. Writers say talking about a book uses it up and you can't write it.

Really?

Do you get books from Amazon.com? asked Marcus.

Well, in Sydney, you know, I could just go to bookshops.

Or I'd read the *New York Review of Books* and ring up Richard and he'd get things for me.

Marcus is always buying books from Amazon, said Kellie. They're pushing us out of the house.

Aren't you supposed to be getting books online? You, of all people. E-books, aren't they called? said Ludmilla, the mayor's wife.

Oh, indeed, said Marcus. But a book is a book. Sometimes I think it is the most perfect creation of the human mind. And heart.

And are you escaping from the rat race, Nissa? asked the mayor.

There's a few of those not a million k from this table, said Gary, who was a solicitor. Escapees, I mean.

You? said Nissa.

Oh, not me, this is home for me. Me father before me and his father afore that. No, this pair. He nodded at Kellie and Marcus.

A microcosm of the IT revolution, said Belinda, who was married to Gary and was a solicitor too. Leaving the city to live in rural bliss and work online.

Any reason for choosing this place?

My family are from hereabouts, said Kellie.

You don't need a genealogical table to live in this town, said Ludmilla, but it helps.

And of course there's the snow, said Kellie. If you like skiing.

I recommend Amazon, said Marcus, if you're keen to get books. Okay, bookshops are great if you can keep getting to town. And Brian in the village has the odd thing. But really, out in the sticks, Amazon is the only way.

I've got to get my computer set up, said Nissa. I haven't even unpacked it yet. I haven't a clue how it works, at all.

Get Marcus out, he's the expert.

Well, we don't usually do that sort of thing . . . we're more . . .

Oh Marcus, just this once, said Kellie. We can be neighbourly, just this once.

That was how it all started. Almost with Kellie's blessing, you could say, but of course you couldn't, Kellie hadn't had an affair in mind when she sent Marcus to set up Nissa's computer, she wanted to secure an interesting friendship. Interesting people weren't that easy to find in small country towns.

Nissa's computer needed a lot of setting up. It kept going wrong. She must have bought a lemon, said Kellie. No, said Marcus, I don't think it's that. It's really that she doesn't understand it. She may be a great cook, but she's not a crash-hot computer operator.

Kellie smiled. Like you, she knew Marcus meant. Though in truth the computers were more him, she was the business side. It didn't occur to her that there might be anything going on. Nissa was much older, and strangely plain, though Kellie had realised that some of her odd dun-coloured clothes were designer labels. Kellie was blond and plump (she'd need to watch it, but so far the word was voluptuous, she said to herself in front of the mirror) and liked the bright-edged colours of ski wear; I enjoy working at home and feeling like a snow bunny, she said. And of course the skiing was close, and they could choose when they took their weekends. When they'd got the business on a good footing they'd start a family, thirty-six wasn't very old, these days. Out of the rat race, in the fresh clean air of the high country.

Maybe I should have a look at it, said Kellie. Maybe there's something you're missing.

I don't think so, though you could have a try, said Marcus, and to Nissa he said, I think this alibi has run out.

There were moments. Kellie went to Canberra for a day. She had her hair cut. Lunch sometimes with Belinda or Jane or Ludmilla. And of course Nissa couldn't get connected to the internet because she didn't have a phone, so she had an excuse to see Marcus and ask him to order books from Amazon.com. She invited the couple to dinner. Oddly plain, said Kellie. Like Nissa herself, really. But delicious, said Marcus. Oh yes, delicious, said Kellie.

But mostly it was Marcus ringing her on the mobile phone.

Where are you?

I'm in bed.

Ah, in bed . . .

Wearing woolly pyjamas and reading Dostoyevsky.

Where are you? The words a little song he always sings, in a cooing breathy voice, but a song he wants to know the answer to.

Sitting on the veranda looking at the paddocks.

Not at work?

You're forgetting—the landscape is why I came to live here. I am learning to be at home in it.

Are you looking upon it with an erotic gaze?

I shall have to think about that. With the eye of desire, perhaps.

Ah, said Marcus. Desire. Yes.

Can one desire landscape?

Isn't that why you came here to live?

Indeed and it was.

Where are you?

Making soup. Out of wild herbs.

Not at the computer? You're never at the computer.

Not when you ring.

In fact Nissa was never at the computer because she wasn't writing the book. Take your time, she said to herself. You need to get your head around it. People assumed it was a recipe book but it wasn't. It was about life, really. The yellow grasslands and the thin slivers of shabby soft drink cases of the Rosalie Gascoigne, the cold old house with its deep brick fires. A son who'd died. Husbands, leaving and left. Reading. Life, really, she said to Marcus, like all the best books. And then wished she hadn't.

Where are you?

Walking in the paddock. Smelling the warm sun in the cold air.

Not at the computer?

Thinking. A book has to be thought, you know.

I'm dying to read it. I wish you'd get it written, I know it's going to be brilliant.

He heard her sharp breath. More than I know, she said.

He didn't ever speak of love or making love or sex or fucking or the performance of their erotic acts or even missing her on the phone. Cordless phones weren't safe, he said. Look what happened to Princess Di. Nissa thought that anyone listening to them talk would know it was the conversation of lovers. The way her voice said some words and then his voice saying his words, and each so very conscious of the other. A woven pattern, like a dance, formal in its steps, and with a stranger or just a friend remaining formal in its intention, but their secret knowing making it sensual as foreplay.

The only time he didn't say, Where are you? was when he muttered, in a hurry, Something's come up, I can't come, I can't meet you, I can't see you.

Does Kellie suspect? she asked.

Oh no, said Marcus, no, I just need to make sure she doesn't.

Nissa thought that Kellie did. This unnatural level of surveillance. But then, of course, deserved.

Hello, Nissa, Marcus here. How are you?

Okay, she said.

Where are you?

I'm going away.

Where?

North. I need somewhere warm. My bones are cold.

Oh.

Don't worry. You can still phone me.

Yes, of course.

Hello, Nissa . . . Where are you?

Ah. I'm sitting at a table under a thatched umbrella drinking real lemonade and in a minute I'm going to have a swim. I'd forgotten how green and blue and beautiful the sea is here.

Oh, he said, his voice husky and yearning. Oh. I wish I were by the sea in the warm sun.

It's hot, she said. Hot.

Are your bones warm yet? he asked.

Soon.

Hello, Nissa. Where are you?

Being very naughty. Sunbathing. Toasting myself. With lots of sunblock on, of course.

What are you wearing?

Not a lot. The bottom half of a bikini.

With only your breasts for company? His voice was jealous.

She laughed.

Wish I was there.

I shall be brown as a berry.

White Nissa, brown as a berry.

Why are berries brown?

Nissa . . . Where are you?

Just about to get into the spa. Relax after a heavy day's lazing round.

A spa? On your own?

Oh Marcus. What do you think?

Don't want to.

I'm fussy who I spa-bath with. Bare all over.

Wish I was there.

I'd spa with you.

And so it went. Nissa was walking along a white beach, with whales disporting offshore. She had swum, was about to swim; had eaten crabs, reef fish, mangos, been snorkelling, not to fish, just to look. A fiery sun had sunk into a red-stained sea. She was drinking white wine that tasted of toast and honey. Eating passionfruit with a silver spoon. The days were languorous, the nights balmy. They have that scent of the tropics, she said, perfumed like a flower. Heady. Dizzy. Swooning.

And Marcus would say, wish I were there, his voice full of yearning. I wish I were there, a holiday is just what I need.

Yes, she said.

Are you collecting material? he asked.

What?

For the book.

Oh, yes, always.

I'm dying to read it.

It's much too soon.

Oh, I do need a holiday. Wish I was there.

Jump on a plane and come up. Why not.

He gave a little groaning laugh. Oh Nissa. You know why not.

Next time he said, wish I was there, she asked: What would you do if you were?

Oh Nissa, not on a mobile phone. You know it isn't safe on a mobile phone. Look at Prince Charles.

Must I, she said.

Nissa . . . Where are you?

I'm sitting by the pool drinking champagne.

Champagne? At this hour?

There's no improper hour for champagne.

I suppose not.

Though it wasn't my idea. My companion insisted.

Companion? Who? A man?

Well, it would hardly be suitable to launch into a detailed description.

Are you sleeping with him?

She laughed. Lovely to talk to you, she said, and pressed the 'end' button.

Nissa, where are you?

Driving up the escarpment. The rainforest is so lush. You can feel it growing.

You shouldn't be talking on the phone while you're driving.

Oh, I'm not. Not driving. She gave a little gurgle of laughter.

Nissa, he said. Again there was that sexy little giggle. He thought it was not meant for him. Nissa, are you coming home soon?

Home? Oh, home.

I do so miss you.

Marcus, you're breaking up.

I do so miss you.

She could hear him shouting. As though shouting could help with breaking up.

Marcus! No good, you're gone. She pressed the 'end' button.

Nissa, where are you?

Oh, she said. Drinking champagne again. On the balcony this time.

With lover boy.

There's a fine turn of phrase.

With lover boy. Lover boy!

It's so warm sitting on the balcony. With a little balmy sea breeze.

Nissa, you're not!

Not what?

You're bloody not! Not sitting on any fucking balcony.

How can you tell me what I'm not doing?

Marcus's voice was climbing octaves. You're not on a balcony drinking champagne. You're bloody well right here.

Well, I know where I am is here.

Here here. On a public bench in this frightful freezing bloody town wearing a great big khaki overcoat.

Taupe.

Right here! And Marcus was standing in front of her, his face bright red and furious, his eyes glaring.

Nissa! When did you get back?

I never went away.

His eyes goggled. You've been here all along?

She nodded.

He sank down on the bench beside her.

You've been lying, he said. You were lying all along. No beach. No champagne. No lover.

No, she said. Champagne. But no beach. No lover, certainly.

Lying, all along.

Lying, she said. It is you who is lying. To yourself. To your wife. To me.

Not to you.

Whereas I am making fictions. You could call them lies. But they are beautiful lies. I was reading Dante, while I was not on my tropical island. Beautiful lies is his phrase. I never knew that. You know what pleasure there is in finishing learning something you half knew? *Bella menzogna*, Dante says. And the thing is, the point is, under the beautiful lie a truth is hidden. A truth lies hidden.

What truth, in this case?

When she didn't answer he went on, speaking in his wounded harsh voice.

You must have known I'd find out sooner or later. Pretty bloody blatant, sitting in the middle of town on a bench.

I only wonder it took you so long. I haven't been hiding. I walked along the main street most days.

I never saw you.

In my big warm overcoat. Taupe. The colour of moles it is, you know. Pretty pinky brown moles.

I never would have suspected you could be so tricky.

No? But you are showing you don't know much about me.

Let's have a cup of coffee. I'm freezing to death.

She shook her head.

No, she said. I did go away. Away from this. She made a fist with her thumb and little finger poking out and held it to her cheek, then pushed her hand into her pocket. I want a lover. Not a man on a cordless phone. All foreplay—and that in code. No climax. That's not enough connection for me. I'm sorry. Phone sex is one thing; I realised we were having phone not-sex.

Only to keep us in touch between making love. We can still do that. Sometimes is better than no times.

She shook her head again. Come to dinner, she said. You and Kellie. I'm cooking some tripe, a recipe rare and spicy, so good you'll wonder why you haven't been eating it all your life. Food for winter and cosy cottages. She smiled. Me, languorous on a beach . . . toasting up a tan. I hate the tropics.

Tripe, he said, I'm not sure Kellie will come at tripe.

Don't tell her. Not till we've eaten it.

## BINGLE

The traffic very thick again. Every morning the traffic very thick. The car going slowly, stopping, crawling forward, stopping. Every morning sitting in a small metal canister, hardly moving. Going from a large canister and the small compartment of her flat in it via an even smaller moving one to a very big official one, full of compartments. Nothing ever happens in a canister, in a compartment of a canister. In a life spent in canisters. Two of them solitary and the third full of people but not in any intimate way. *Hello, how are you today, take off your clothes above the waist and put this robe on.* Then making them be naked and stand at the machine. Only women, of course. Her job to take hold of their breasts and flatten them, spreading them on the metal of the machine, pressing them out. Pressing down on them. Like hamburgers, Tania thought. Kneading, spreading. Pressing. Knowing you hurt them, because it isn't mincemeat that you are dealing with but living flesh.

Her colleagues were okay, very nice really, but running in and out of their own lives. Maybe a tired coffee, a chat. Children ill, husbands lazy, mothers dementing. Friendly but not friends. Lunchtime going for a walk, looking at clothes she couldn't afford to buy, not with the mortgage on the flat.

I ought to change something, Tania said to herself as the traffic stopped again. A life spent in various sized canisters, metal and otherwise, is no life. Catch the bus? Another metal canister. With other people. But would they be company? Buses she'd been on they were all zombies, closed in by their iPods, staring with shuttered eyes refusing any contact.

Get a job doing mammograms in Italy. Why not. She had no idea if it would be possible, probably not. Getting there would be another metal canister, twenty-four hours of it this time. But then a small town somewhere, where people would be patient with her halting Italian. With bountiful meals under grape-shaded arbours. That was in the photographs; it was quite likely life wouldn't be like that. Whenever does real life resemble a lifestyle photograph?

The traffic moved forward. It looked as though she might get through the lights. But the car ahead inexplicably stopped and from accelerating she had to brake suddenly. There was a violent jolt that snapped her against the seatbelt and shook the breath out of her, making her slow to realise someone had run into the back of her car.

She got out. There was a tall man with a brown carved face which looked as if it should be enfolded in white woollen robes above a body galloping on a fine thoroughbred through the desert. He was gibbering with rage. Lots of *fucking*s, and *my god my car* many times. One *stupid cunt*, three *bloody criminals* and at least five *female moron drivers*. Three *my beautiful car*s and two *my beautiful blue BMW*s. Several *heaps of shit* and one *buggered beyond repair*. His accent didn't sound like a man on a thoroughbred in the desert but maybe he'd been to a good boarding school. So rich these people were.

As far as Tania could see, standing disoriented by the shock of the impact and bemused by the flow of invective that was washing over her, there was hardly a mark on his car, while hers had the bumper torn half off and crushed into a back wheel.

It's your fault, she said.

What?

It's your fault.

He gibbered some more: *morons, fucking women telling lies*.

It's always the fault of the person behind who runs into the person in front, said Tania.

If you hadn't stopped so stupidly . . .

I'd have run into the car in front. I didn't. You ran into me. It's your fault. We'll get the police.

He leaned towards her and she bent backwards from her pliant waist as if he was about to scoop her up on his trusty steed and gallop off into the film of the man on the thoroughbred in the desert, the violent foul-mouthed aggressive man used to having his own way. She bent back from her pliant waist and then in a neat little spiral movement slid to the ground. He stood astride, glaring down at his prey lying at his feet.

Hang on, said Tania. I wouldn't say that.

What? I spoke crossly. There was a flow going, I didn't want to lose it.

All that about tin boxes.

Tin . . . ? Oh, the metal canisters.

Metal . . . whatever. I wouldn't say it. I'd have the music on. Red Hot Chili Peppers it was today. The music on, you're in the moment, you're not thinking about tin . . .

Canisters.

Canisters, whatever. You're listening to the music. There was home, there'll be work, but why would you think about them? You know the traffic's slow, it always is, so why fuss? You've allowed enough time and the Red Hot Chili Peppers are playing . . .

You're supposed to be wanting a change.

Yeah, well, I've got one, haven't I. Buggered car.

His insurance will pay.

He might scarper, since I seem to have passed out.

Well, I'm not planning to leave you there, it's just that you're distracting me. Anyway, there's quite a crowd gathered. All the people whose cars are stuck behind yours. They won't let him run away.

Is my car drivable?

Probably we can bend the bumper back. It'll be okay till you get it to the garage.

That tyre's looking pretty wrecked. Might be better to get it towed. Then he can give me a lift.

What? Don't be silly. He's a nasty man, full of road rage. And his language—I can hardly bring myself to transcribe it.

I like his carved brown face. He looks as though he should be wrapped in white woollen robes on a thoroughbred in the desert. An Arab steed. I'm sure he's got a house full of Persian carpets and that copperware with the silver worn off.

What are you talking about? That face was there for contrast. Unexpected, in the context. I'm not writing a fantasy out of a Rudolph Valentino movie.

Why not? When you've got the chance. Another thing. All that business of boobs like hamburgers. Yuck. I nearly lost my breakfast. A breast is a respectful thing. Mammograms are an important service for women. They save lives. Not much fun but very serious.

They hurt like hell.

So what. No pain no gain.

I hate people talking in clichés.

Tania glared at me and went into a sulk.

I suppose, I said, I had some idea of women as, well, as meat.

Not in mammograms. Anyway, who's talking in clichés now?

More of an archetype, I said. Tania was still sulking. You wouldn't really get a lift with him?

Of course.

He's violent. He's aggressive.

Only verbally. I like powerful men. When my soft violet eyes looked into his piercing black ones . . .

You haven't got violet eyes!

I can if I want to. My violet eyes. His black ones. Sparks flew.

Eech.

You said I wanted something to happen. So it has.

Yes, but that was irony. That wasn't what you wanted to happen. That was life, you wishing for something interesting to change it and bingo it clobbers you with some stupid event that just fucks you up.

I get to meet a gorgeous hunk of man, said Tania. What's wrong with that?

It was my turn to sulk. The girl-meets-boy-by-means-of-car-accident narrative is as dead as the dodo, I said.

Bullshit. By the way, haven't I been lying on the road in

a faint for rather a long time? said Tania. Fortunately I am wearing my leather miniskirt with the lace-top stay-up black sheer stockings and the skirt has slid up to show a sliver of milky white thigh. Or should that be creamy white thigh?

To do *mammograms*?

Why not? Got to have a bit of fun somewhere. At least I'm wearing Hush Puppies, not stilettos. Cute little red Mary Jane Hush Puppies.

You can't afford leather miniskirts with your mortgage.

Tania wiped her eyes on a eucalyptus-smelling tissue. Sadly, my dad died last year. I was really sorry even though I hadn't seen him since I was knee-high to a grasshopper, but it was a great help on the mortgage front. And I'm learning Italian, I should have enough money to go there soon.

I did remember writing that she was thinking of going to Italy to work. I said, Do you think that's going to happen?

It might, if you got my slender long-legged body up off the ground. Look at my yellow corn-silk hair fanning across the bitumen. Couldn't he at least fold up his jacket and put it under my head?

What's corn silk?

Don't you know anything? That straight silky stuff you get on sweet corn, under the leaves, you pull it off before you wrap the cobs in cling wrap and microwave them. It means fine straight blond hair. Naturally.

Nothing too natural about it, I wouldn't think.

If you've got the right genes it is.

What about a mop of red curls?

Isn't that a bit Enid Blyton?

You're too young to have grown up with Enid Blyton.

No I'm not. What's with this stereotyping? You're so judgmental.

It's not stereotyping to notice that man's violent. Not the jacket-under-the-head type at all.

Well, she said, her voice impatient. At least get me up off the ground.

In a minute. You and road-rage man . . .

He's an orthopaedic surgeon, by the way.

Oh please.

What's his name?

Emile.

Ooh, I don't care for that. What about Tony?

You and . . . Tony exchange addresses and insurance companies. The ambulance comes and takes you to the hospital, you have to be checked out in case there's a compo claim.

I feel fine. I just came over a bit giddy from the scent of his aftershave. Eau Sauvage. I love Eau Sauvage on a man. He says he'll give me a lift to work. In his sparkling new blue BMW with cream leather seats. Black convertible top. He phones his secretary and tells her to cancel his clients—

—patients—

—for the day—

—irresponsible as well as a road rager—

—and phones in sick for me. We drive to Sydney, it's such a good way to talk, he says, to really get to know one another, we need to talk, we have so much to say. He puts on the Red Hot Chili Peppers ever so softly, and off we go.

In a small metal canister all the way to Sydney.

We have lunch at, where? Tetsuya's? Quay? Bilson's? He'll know the best place.

What a pity you've got a horrible big hole in your black sheer lace-top stay-up stockings.

I always carry a spare pair in my Hermès Kelly bag.

Now you're being ridiculous.

A present from my last boyfriend, the merchant banker. He wanted to marry me but I said no. He was lovely and rich but a bit dull.

Oh excellent. You've got a great imagination. So, what happens next?

Tony fell in love with me when he saw me lying helpless on the ground—my corn-silk hair spread across the bitumen. We get married and have four children and live happily ever after.

You can't marry a man who gibbers at a perfect stranger after a car accident that was his fault.

Oh, that was an aberration. He'd just lost a very dear patient and wasn't himself.

Criminal negligence, I shouldn't wonder.

He did everything he could. He'd kept him alive for years, everybody said it was a miracle, but death defeated him in the end.

Orthopaedic surgeons come in, cut, saw, and disappear in a puff of huge bill.

You're so cynical. Tony is a true healer.

Tania, I can't write this. It's . . . it's . . . banal. And the oh-so-neat happy ending. I don't do closure.

All the more reason for doing something different for once. Change, remember, we were wanting a change. You're the one in the rut.

I could see she was tough, this girl. No talking to her. She stared at me with her fierce eyes. Violet? Maybe.

So, she said. What were you going to do with me?

I hadn't worked it out, yet.

What? You mean you started writing me and didn't know where you were going?

The story knows where it's going. I start writing and I find out. The story knows.

Well, that's me. I'm trying to tell you.

No, you're a character, you're not the story, it's the story that has its own life. You have rather a pedestrian mind, but the narrative can still be quite original. With its own sense of menace.

Tania sighed. I don't want menace. I want happiness. You're a writer, you know about love at first sight. I can't live without him.

Tania, he's a monster. He'll beat you and the children. He'll probably kill you. In fact that's where the story might have been going.

Killing me? Killing?

Yeah, but I don't like that much. A bit simple. Look, we've got to get you up off the road. That's a big faint you're in. What happens: the ambulance comes, takes you to the hospital, gets you checked out. Possible compensation, remember.

He's an orthopaedic surgeon, remember. He'll look after me.

I don't think so. He's actually the son of a drug dealer, that's where the car came from. He's actually a kind of ne'er-do-well—

Ne'er-do-well? Is this the 1930s we're in?

Even a bit of a psychopath. Definitely a psychopath. I can't let you get into a car with this man. Let alone drive to Sydney.

It doesn't have to be like this. Write him nicer. A surgeon. A healer. Falling in love at first sight. You can, you know.

I shook my head. You get taken to the hospital. You come to, out of your faint, and exchange addresses. You're very weak, you've had a traumatic experience, don't forget, the collision, and all that shouting, and maybe you hit your head when you fell. They'll keep you in overnight for observation. And this man, he really is a nasty piece of work, he starts to stalk you, it's terrible, the story turns into a kind of thriller at that point, will you survive, or will he take you to his McMansion in O'Malley and . . . though maybe that's a bit melodramatic, not my style either, really; I need to subvert it somehow . . . What I need is a bit of peace and quiet to find out where we're going.

Tania stuttered with rage. You're the monster. Why can't it be nice? Why can't it be true love and marriage and children and happy ever after?

It's not my genre. I have to do real life, not romance. My kind of stories—they're not happy ever after. They need anxiety. Unease. Menace.

Novels end happily.

After a lot of vicissitudes. Even Mills and Boon have vicissitudes. Whereas a short story doesn't really have room for them. A short story is just one vicissitude, in a manner of speaking.

So why do I have to be a short story?

I suppose I could do a novel . . . about a mammographer and an orthopaedic surgeon in a blue BMW? It'd need a lot of subversion.

A novel would be good. I think I need a novel to get me all in. And Annabelle and Nathaniel and . . .

Who're they?

The children.

I'm not really into a novel. And I don't do children. What I've got in mind is a short story, rather bleak, variations on the image of the metal capsule, a sad sharp tale about the ambiguities of wishes, the potential terror of their coming true. Lots of ironies.

Sounds extremely miserable to me. I reckon irony is more fun to do than be.

Okay, Tania, I said. You don't faint. He leans towards you, in your face, you bend backwards from your pliant waist. As I keep saying, he's not a nice man, despite the BMW. In fact he gives you a shove, and you fall and hit your head on a sharp piece of your buckled rear end. The ambulance takes you to hospital.

Sorry, Tania—no argument. At least you've got private health insurance, you should get a room to yourself. And I'll get you some grapes. Grapes are such a cliché in hospitals that they're really an ironic statement all by themselves. Grapes are a nice touch.

The ambulance men slide her on to the stretcher and click it up to its standing position. She does look beautiful, with her fair hair and the lovely domed curve of her violet eyelids. They tuck the red blanket over her. Heavens . . . they aren't pulling it up over her face—are they? I didn't mean to delete her. She only wanted happiness with a man who loved her. Don't we all. No mammograms and a man to love us. Well, more comfortable mammograms. Tania would have been a nice person to do it, if you had to have a mammogram. For god's sake, stop being sentimental, woman. Remember you're a serious writer. Still, maybe if I go back I could . . . No, you know it'll never work . . . Oh good, it's okay, they're just tucking her in, she's not dead. Cover her face: it's poignant that the covering of the face means death. I'll make sure she gets a good swag of flowers in the hospital—maybe resurrect the merchant banker. He'd be a better bet than road rager here. Dull, but it's caring that counts.

The ambulance pulls away and drives sedately down the road. The man, Tony—Emile would be a better name—has been pacing up and down beside his BMW, his carved brown face scowling. It could indeed be enfolded in flowing white wool. Then you'd fear he would be about to order your execution if you displeased him overnight. Or even if you didn't; a night of love then off with her head. Suddenly he jumps in the car, it starts instantly, sweetly, he revs the engine, reverses sharply back with a crunch into the car behind, and then swerves out into the road, accelerating as he goes. The lights are red, he races through the intersection, weaving his way through the cars streaming across it, hitting two, bouncing off a third, rolling twice, screeching across the bitumen and crunching to a stop against the pole of the red traffic light. The shining blue paint shimmers, it crinkles and crazes, it's a crumple of metal, hardly blue and not shining any more. How fast this happens to a car. He wasn't wearing the seatbelt, he lies on the ground beside it, the airbag balloons uselessly; his body . . . the policemen, who have run the short distance from the bingle to the terrible crash, shake their heads.

As the car rolled its boot sprang open. Seven slim attaché cases were flung out and cast over the road. One popped open and small brown paper packets flew out. The policemen transfer their attention from the disarticulated body on the road, hardly even bleeding now, to the attaché cases and the packets. Their faces are full of glee, however long they pull them they can't disguise that.

I told Tania he was a drug dealer. Sitting in the hospital eating her grapes she can consider she's had a lucky escape. It need not have come at such a price, but it was clear from the beginning that he was a nasty piece of work. And not very bright. That sinister dumb arrogance. Ugly characters, even more than nice ones, have minds of their own. They will have their way.

Though the fate of the narrative won't always let them.

I'll go back to the bingle. The story isn't actually about that—the bingle is just the agent of change, horrible expression, I mean the way to get things going . . . And maybe Tania meets her loving doctor in the hospital. But I don't need to write that.

## TOGETHER FOREVER

He said we should take all our clothes off and just be together. He said that was what God wanted, it was innocent and pure, like Adam and Eve in the Garden before there was any sin, it was all beautiful and pure and innocent and that was what God always wanted for people. I felt shy, I wouldn't have minded a couple of months ago when my chest was quite flat when I could look at myself without any top and feel free like any child a boy even but now there are little bumps, I think they are like tiny volcanoes pushing their cones through the surface of my skin and they feel hot and itchy as if they might erupt and hot lava come running out. I don't look at his body though I get a feel of muscle and especially down there, I have never thought of it before but it is as if some strong muscle springing out though I haven't looked. I look at his face the other girls in the hostel say they can see a halo round his head when he is saying prayers standing by the altar in his shining white robes, look at Father they say, a glow like little flames around his hair and when I lie beside him that is what I see, a glow around his head and beaming at me through his eyes. This is what God wants he says, for us to be together, just lying and touching not doing it yet the way a husband and wife do, but when I am fifteen we will we will be husband and wife in God's sight. We are lying on a rug of foxes' skins he shot the foxes himself they are pale gold and silky but then they prickle a bit too on my bare bottom and my itchy little bumps when he makes me wriggle.

He strokes me his fingers are thrilling scooping down my spine and around my bottom and sometimes slipping just in there, how wet he says, my juicy little love and I think it must be wee but of course it isn't I could stop that and this is just coming. I think of dripping sticky on the foxes' fur but he doesn't seem to mind. There is beginning to grow a little bit of hair down there it is reddish too like the fox he says, my foxy love, not like the hair on my head which is really just pale brown.

He writes letters and tells me how he loves me, how we are meant to be together, how we will never be parted. He tells me how beautiful I am but I know I am not, girls always know who the beautiful ones are in the class and who the pretty ones are and who the attractive ones that the boys all notice and I know I am none of those things. He tells me it is

God's will that he should love me and I think he must be right because how would it happen otherwise? I look at the photo he took of me and Lynette and the other girls at the pool and I cannot see how I am not very plain, my eyes squinting up and my face like a bun and Lynette not much better, but a couple of the girls have bones and shadows in the right place and you could think of them being film stars, their bumps bigger than mine too, not that I want big bumps I would rather be my old flat self.

I keep the letters in a box, a sort of cane box that Auntie Joan gave me to be a sewing basket, it has red satin inside and I have made a slit in the bottom to slide the letters in. It is important to be secret, one day everybody will know and we will be husband and wife in the eyes of the world as well as of God but it is too soon yet. There is also a book about things that married couples do though I don't really need it since he shows me he says I am good my soft body is so pliable his wife does not do these things she does not understand him what a man needs not the way I do. In the letters he tells me all the things we will do they make me feel hot and churned up inside, the letters are like the things in the book but better because they are about me. The words stay in my head and I think of them when he puts the bread in my mouth when I am kneeling at the altar rail. I look at him there now since I have to put a french letter on him I must not get pregnant yet though he is dying for me to have his child and suckle him as he suckles my bumps the little volcanoes growing bigger pushing their cones further out of my skin. I think it is me doing this he says laughing I am sucking them out. Of course there is no milk in them yet. I suck him too like an ice cream before I put the french letter on of course it is not at all like ice cream it really is a kind of muscle it is so strong and it has its own mind. Seeking you out, he says, looking for his love. It is called Felix which means happy he says. Felix tells me he is missing you he whispers in the playground and I feel the churned-up feel. I have got a name down there too it is Pussy.

It seems to be taking a long time for God to choose the moment that is ripe for us but he says God knows what he is doing we have to be patient and trust His will. The girls are all in love with him. They do not know he is in love with me. We are secret in his study on the fox-skin rug. They swoon and go on about his halo to themselves. They wish they were his wife, they think she is rather ugly, what can he see in her. Look at her nose they say, how can Father be married to a nose like that? I say his halo is golden like a fox's tail. You mean brush says Lynette, you are silly Ros, that is not what a halo is. It is quite lonely in the hostel even with the other girls it is not like your own family, your mother and father.

I notice that his wife is getting fat and then one day I see that it is not fat it is a baby. She already has two and how can this baby have got in there since it is me he loves, me who is husband and wife with him and it is as if somebody has punched me in the chest, punched me hard where my heart is and knocked all the air out, I can't breathe and I slide to the ground bumping my back on the pew and the world spins and goes dark. They must drag me outside because in a while I am sitting on a bench under the peppermint gum with my head between my legs. So hot in there says the matron, and the wife murmurs She is probably outgrowing her strength, they do at that age, Well, says Matron I suppose teenage girls do have a habit of fainting. I know it is my heart that has been punched nearly to death and will never recover from this splitting pain but I don't say so.

There are a lot of letters now and I have to find another place, the bulge in the red satin lining is too big. I put them in the bottom of the box I keep schoolwork in. We do a lot of written work, compositions, history essays, French proses, nobody will ever look underneath this pile of marked and forgotten work. You are the love of my life he says we will be together forever and Felix will be forever with his lovely Pussy the words pale blue on the crinkly page. He gets me to babysit the new baby and I pull up my school uniform and put him to one of my bumps and he sucks just like his father, I think this baby knows I should be his mother. I wonder would milk come if he sucked long enough but he pretty soon notices there isn't any and stops.

This evening Lynette and I walk into town and go to the pictures and there are some boys there who talk to us.

Afterwards we go and have a milkshake. They seem nice boys, a bit quiet, we ask them what they thought of the film but they haven't really got anything to say, they live on farms some way out of town and used to go to boarding school but they are finished now. They say they will drive us home and the one in the back seat tries to hold Lynette's hand and after a bit she lets him but the boy with me in the front seat is driving, it's his father's car. When we get back to the hostel Father is waiting for us, he shouts at us, tells Lynette to get inside and then takes me to his study, I am in mortal danger he says and he is sending me home.

My parents frown and stare at me, home in disgrace, that a daughter of ours should turn out a slut they say. I can't tell them about Father and they don't believe me about the boys, that we just had a milkshake and got driven home. I didn't even hold his hand I say, but they turn their heads away and snap their teeth, That's not the message we've been given, young lady. Pity about your education, says my mother, you might have made something of yourself. Dad shakes his head. Didn't I always say, education, it's a waste of time for a girl.

Twenty years, it will be soon, with Mal. Twenty years, it's too long. I thought he might look after me but it's all just harm. Now I think I've got to get the kids out. Two've gone, one to Sydney, Valerie the eldest, to the bank, Dan down Victoria way to the river boats. Funny, a kid all his life in this dry inland and boats are all he cares about. I'm happy, Mum, he says in a postcard, and I think, this is a message. My son is telling me, there is happiness. And that night when Mal comes in drunk and knocks me about, nothing new in that, I'm used to it, but then when the youngest chimes in, Leave her alone, Dad, he says, you're a bully, and Mal fetches him a dirty great wallop over the ear so he sprawls up against the hearth, his eyes closed, and I think he's dead, he's broken his neck, he's going to be a quadriplegic, he'll be a vegetable, and I pick Colin's limp body up in my arms and just stare at Mal and he slopes off, grinding his teeth that all these bastard kids and the bitch wife will be the death of him, bastard kids he says when they're all born decently in wedlock and christened too, but wedlock in truth, chained up and shut away and tortured. That night I say to myself we are leaving.

So limp his little body is and cold, should he be so cold? He is thin, all my children are thin it is as though they do not thrive and yet they are healthy wiry tough Dan on his river boat so young but I am happy Mum he says and now here is Colin and maybe he is dead but he sniffles and then his eyes open and he sees me, Are you all right Mum he says and tries to get up, What about you son I say, I'm tired he says, We'll get you to bed I say, and I stay with him, perhaps it is concussion, you have to stay with children with concussion, make sure they do not go dead asleep. His sister comes to see what is happening and I send her back to bed, she knows better than to come out when her father is on one of his rampages but now it is all quiet, most like he has passed out. It is okay I say but I am thinking it is not and hasn't been and now I must do something and then I think I will write to the bishop, Father is a bishop now, I read it in the *Women's Weekly*. I might have made something of myself if I hadn't been sent home, *expelled* is the word, before I could get my School Certificate but then there was only the job in the draper's until along came Mal and the farm, he seemed nice then, and me lucky to get him, a girl with a reputation sent home from the hostel. The *Women's Weekly* tells you about the world and I see Father is a bishop, up north, now he has six children, there he is with his wife smiling out of the picture, he is a good bishop people talk about all the good things he does with young people and homeless as well as standing there in purple with fancy embroidery, his wife is a brown bird and he is the peacock.

I get out his old letters tied into little bundles with red ribbons for true love, kept hidden all these years from Mal in the box the toaster came in. Not my letters he would not let me write any too dangerous but reading his takes me back to the time when love was and I write to him from then and now.

And here we are back they come pale blue words on the crinkly page, it is the same, I am his love and he must be with me. After the letters he comes and takes me away not to our local town but much further away where no one knows us, we will be together soon it is God's will for us. He sends presents. A necklace made of carved and polished bone. A ring with a big red stone. The fox rug. It smells of mothballs now and the skins are a bit dried and cracked. The fur is as good as ever he says, look at these silky brushes the foxes that I shot myself, he smooths them with his hand, the playground of our love he calls it, living again, he strokes my breasts and slides his fingers down the knobs of my spine, I feel as though I am a harp he is playing. My lovely girl, he whispers. He will come to us when he can, he says, for now just sometimes, but when it is God's will forever together. We will have our baby he says.

It is a secret from Mal where we are. It would be a good idea for him to know so there could be money for the children, but he might come after us.

And now I am happy for the first time since being a child. Father I can call him Roy all the time now Roy is with me it is the time he says, it is God's will. We are having picnics. The pain from the past might be going away. But then there are telephone calls and the church sends a light plane and he goes away just for a little while to sort it out. More letters crinkly blue on the white paper. He is coming. Soon.

I write a letter telling him I am having his baby which he wants me to carry and suckle for him so then he writes and says he can't come back his wife is upset and he hopes I find someone to support me.

I read the *Women's Weekly*. I wear the ring with the red

stone. The baby kicks in my womb, so full of life this baby. On the television there is a program about homeless children and there is my bishop slowly kissing the hand of his plain brown wife, she looks up at him over her nose it is pretty big and smiles at him, he turns and looks at the camera, he says, You know, the most important thing I ever did in my life was marry this lady.

One day there's a pain and a lot of blood and no baby any more. I suppose I am too old now for a baby to work. I have never had a mis before.

I try to make a happy life but I can't. The three younger children grow up and go into lives of their own. I try studying at TAFE, going overseas and starting again, but it doesn't work. I look at the letters. You are the love of my life, they say. I write to him. I am too old, he says. I can't be at this kind of thing any more.

Forty years I am thinking it is now, since I was a child lying on a fox rug with itchy bumps on her chest rubbing prickly in the red brushes of foxes. If he is too old now I was too young then.

All the letters. A lifetime of letters, interrupted but going on over the years in their own way. And the photographs. The steps of the hostel and me fourteen years old with a face like a bun. Cute I was I must suppose. His letters say it is me, so special me, me he loves. They say Felix loves Pussy. I take them in their bundles with red ribbons to the bishop, the new one, now my bishop has retired living at the beach with his plain brown wife, grey she is now. I have carried them with me all alone for too many years. The new bishop says he cannot believe his eyes. Sick, he says. Sick. One sick puppy.

He goes to higher authorities who are shocked and cannot believe so good a man a priest but there it is in pale blue words rubbing away and crumpling. The newspapers find out. They offer me money for my story. No I say, not now, this is not about money. But they get stories anyway, and pictures, of then and now, so I do talk to them, since the truth is what we want.

Defrocked, my old bishop is. All the lovely robes, gone. All the godly clothes, taken off. Disgraced. *Expelled*. Living still at the beach. With his wife standing by him.

What worries me, though. If he wanted to come back, I am afraid I might let him. I say no, to myself, but I don't know. Together forever. Forever together. Yes.

## WHAT ABOUT THE SPIDER?

What about the spider?

Pardon?

The spider. The spider's point of view. Have you ever thought of that?

The woman comes into the tent, hesitant, brave; you can see the tension that is screwing her up to this bravery, the coiled fingers, the tremors in her bare arms. She gestures, to the tent, which is only a roof and one wall, to the table, the chairs, a gesture that means, is it all right for me to come here . . . ?

I gesture back, to the chair, where she sits, to the tray of fruit, watermelon in triangles, slices of peach, orange rings, blood red halves of plums. Refreshment for a hot day. She sits, shakes her head to the fruit.

I thought, maybe it was just for the writers, she says.

And visitors, I reply.

Well. She sits still for a moment. Well, I wanted to say, in my case I'm the spider, and I don't think I'm a bad person, have you ever thought of writing from the spider's point of view?

She's just been to a workshop on a novel of mine, the one called *Spider Cup*, about a woman whose husband tells her he's fallen in love with a much younger person and is leaving her, his wife, and the group was talking about this young woman being a spider with hairy legs who's drawn the husband to her and is clutching him tight with these sticky hairy legs. The women, they were nearly all women at the workshop, laughed with malice, they liked this image of a predatory young husband stealer. They could see the word as a kind of revenge.

The thing is, I say to my visitor, the book's about the wife, so it's from her point of view, and naturally she sees the girl like that. She might not be right, but it's her book, so that's the way she shows the situation to us. We don't get the girl's point of view, and we don't get the husband's either.

I'm racking my brains. I do write about adulteries a lot, I know, but do I ever do it from the point of view of the other, the third, the one who, when you come to think of it, makes the story? She's the agent in the narrative of the couple but she has her own tale as well. I can't think of any times I've told it, but then I do have a bad memory for things I've written. It's as though writing them is what counts, and then I let them go, forget them.

It's a good question, I say, and now you've brought it up maybe I'll do it.

She's sitting straight in her chair, her knees and ankles together, her arms straight in her lap, her hands clasped. Outside the sun is shining on emerald green lawn and on the gently flowing river which is emerald coloured too, and very beautiful if you don't think about the green being algae. You wouldn't drown if you fell into it, someone says, it would poison you first. Nevertheless, it flows very prettily, with languid lapping ripples, between its green grass banks, the willows, the dappling gums. Even knowing it is poisonous I think it is beautiful.

The woman is rather good-looking, with clear rosy skin and that silky thick nearly white hair that comes from going grey young. I don't think I'm a bad person, she says again. She wants to tell me her story. When people want to tell you something they are very strong, their will holds you. She is determined that I will hear her spider narrative. Tellers of their own stories are all ancient mariners, they don't let you get away.

Nineteen years she's been with this man, she says. Nineteen years.

It's a long time. I think, so it's a story about an albatross, too.

He always said he wouldn't break up his family, she says. She knew that from the start, he's never pretended otherwise.

When I ask about children, she nods. Yes, there are children. It turns out he has three children with his wife, two with her.

That's two families, really, I say. So how old are the children? She tells me the wife's are twenty-one, twenty-four and twenty-eight, hers are seven and four. I say that the wife's children are grown-up, they should be leading their own lives, it wouldn't be wrecking a family now, what about his family with her? Doesn't he owe them something?

It's his wife, she says. It would be hard for her, he doesn't want to hurt her.

I mention a friend of mine who has children about the same age as the wife's. She fell in lust (she called it) with someone else and had passionate times with him and thought that would be all there was to it, fantastic sex, but then she fell in love with him too; her husband's pride was hurt when she left but now he's found someone else, although the new woman thinks the orchestras on his CDs are awful. But he can cope with that.

The sex isn't good, she says, the sex is lousy.

Nineteen years, I think, and lousy sex.

The thing is, she says, he doesn't want to betray his wife.

But he is, isn't he, he's betraying her and he's betraying you: I think this, but I say, She doesn't know, then?

Oh no. No.

Do you ever think of . . . telling her? Letting her, maybe, find out?

No. She clutches herself round her elbows. If she found

out she'd be round on my doorstep . . . She shakes her head, gives a shiver.

You mean you think she'd harm you?

Me, her husband, herself. She'd do a lot of damage. He's about to become mayor, she says.

I think of revenge. A big scandal and beautiful disgrace for the new mayor.

Do you know the wife?

Oh yes. I know her. She knows me.

And she doesn't suspect anything?

No.

I wonder. Not aloud. Do you live here? I ask, looking out at the green view, the white buildings where the festival is being held. It's quite something for a place this size to manage a literary festival.

No, she says, and names a place further down the coast. About seventy kilometres away. People come from all over the region to this festival.

Later, when I tell this story to Jill, while we're sitting in the airport lounge waiting for planes home, she says, Well, maybe the wife doesn't know but I bet she's the only person in the whole town who doesn't. Do you know how small that place is? Tiny. Much much smaller than here.

She doesn't believe anybody knows.

She could be mistaken. Or, have you thought, she might be making it all up?

I look at Jill.

Knowing how interested in narratives you are. Giving you a present of this story, and tricking you at the same time. Somehow generously cheating you.

I suppose it's possible. But I don't believe it. She was so tentative, so tremulous, so keyed up. You can't fake those things. I'm sure she was honest, I say. You know how people say, painfully honest? That's what she was. It was so important to her. An immense secret, and she couldn't bear not to tell someone, and I was from far away, and it would be safe.

Secrets are never safe with writers.

They turn them into fiction, and that's safe.

Maybe, says Jill, she tells you this tragic story so that you'll make it public, a grand and glorious catastrophe, and that will save her.

She does need saving. The more I hear of her story, the more that becomes clear.

She says, I'm thinking of getting out, finishing.

I nod. Maybe the expression on my face is the kind that would let you describe it as wise. I'm doing sums. Nineteen years, and the eldest child seven. Whose decision? I bet not his. Mister greedy cake-eater cake-keeper. She's pretty and smooth-faced, but I bet she thought she was getting to her last chance of having kids. Biological clocks ticking, and all that. Ask not for whom the clock ticks, et cetera. I wish it ticked for lover boy. Like Captain Hook's crocodile, biding its time, never forgetting.

Do you see any villains in all this? I ask.

She shrugs. I remember that she came looking for me to tell me that she wasn't, that the spider wasn't necessarily the wicked one.

Do you have a career? I ask. I'm shocking myself a bit with this conversation, at the frankness of the questions I'm asking, of their rudeness. The tension of her body, the delicate tight springing of it, is asking for my honesty. We have bypassed politeness, or rather, pared it away. There are things I don't pry after, like her name. I imagine she doesn't want to tell me her name. I'd expect it to be elegant, like Diana, or Caroline. Helen perhaps.

Yes, she says, I'm a vet.

I smile, I'm delighted, excited. That's great, I say. You've got something really interesting to do.

I'm not practising. Not since the children.

I don't ask where the money comes from. But you could go back to it, I say.

Oh yes.

If I were telling this story, not her, I'd feel I had some explaining to do: the small place, the vet who suddenly stops work and has two children. What's gossip doing with this? Who can it think is the father? Small towns are cesspits where secrets fester.

I say: What does . . . does the wife have a job? What does he do in life?

They run a business together.

I wish now I'd asked what the business was. Such reticence in the midst of frankness; looking back I think of course she controlled that. Later I try to imagine. Is he a butcher, and his wife helps in the shop? Wrapping up the meat he cuts with his endlessly sharpened knife. That seems old-fashioned, like being a grocer, but it is a very small town. A pub? A service station? A card and greeting shop? What kind of job does a man do that takes him on to getting himself made mayor? Anything's possible, I suppose, except that you think wanting to be mayor means you'd be a certain sort of person which means you'd be doing a certain kind of job. Public spirited, ambitious, greedy . . . If I were writing this story as fiction—which I am sure my spider wants me to do, she wants me to write an account of how a good woman, an honest woman, a sensible woman, gets to spend nineteen years of her life as mistress of a man who isn't even any good at sex and not much better it seems at loving—if I were fleshing out her life as fiction I'd have to invent his business for him and I can't imagine what it can be. Don't forget it has to allow him time to see her, so his wife doesn't suspect. Flower farming? Does she make something and he delivers it? Jam, perhaps, *Mrs McGinty's Home Made Preserves*, and he's on the road selling it, but not as long as she thinks. Maybe it's a bookshop. But the town would be too small. A newsagency perhaps, and he delivers the papers, and isn't home sleeping as she thinks while she minds the shop.

Do you ever wish she were dead, I ask, that she dies in her sleep, say? For in my novel the wife spends quite a lot of time slitting the wrists and ankles of the other woman and letting her bleed to death in the forests of the mind, as she puts it, and why shouldn't my spider woman fantasise too?

I think of her getting run over by a bus, she says. I laugh.

But, she goes on, he wouldn't come and live with me, even so, even if he was free.

Why not?

He's a loner.

I don't laugh, I snort. This two-familied man, a loner?

I think it would a good idea to break with him, I say, the right thing. Then I put my hand over my mouth and make horrified eyes at her. Look, I say, I'm sorry, I shouldn't have said that, people should never give people advice. Even when they know them. Sorry, pretend I didn't say that. I can't possibly say anything about the situation. I don't know you, I don't know it.

I'd like to say, there are other men, kind men, who'll love you and not cheat you, but I can't, I'd like to think so, I've known some, but they seem to have got pretty thin on the ground and maybe there aren't any at all where she is, otherwise why spend time with this one? When she leaves him it will almost certainly have to be for herself, respect for herself and faith that she can manage, with the help of a good profession and her own courage, not transferring the responsibility to someone else.

I bought your book, she says, I thought it might help me.

I don't think it will, the spider in that just disappears, stops being relevant. But I don't say that, I say I'll remember what she says, I'll write something from the point of view of . . . the point of view she's suggested, I can see there's a lot to be said.

I wonder if I ought to offer to sign the book for her but decide she mustn't want me to, otherwise she'd ask. I can see she's talked to me enough, I've still got a mass of questions but she wants to go; I shake her hand and wish her well. She walks firmly away through the green afternoon, a slender bare-armed woman in a straight white linen dress showing her nice round bottom that rolls just a little as she walks.

I could give her and her lover and her children and her lover's wife names and places to live and habits and words in their mouths, but I think I won't, I'll leave her in her handful of facts, anonymous. But maybe one day there'll be a woman in a story who's not just an agent in a dicey marriage but a narrative herself. In a white dress, with soft white silky hair and a tentative smile. And in the meantime, maybe the lover's wife will read these bare bones and recognise them—though the town she lives in isn't seventy kilometres from the literary festival, I changed that—and . . . well, what?

Maybe that's what the mistress, the spider woman, wants, not so much the wife finding out but using me to put an end to it. She's made a story of it and given it away. Maybe now she can write her own ending. I'd be inclined to go for catastrophe and utter dénouement, but maybe she will just stop.

It's much later that it occurs to me that at no time does either of us mention her love for the man. Why didn't I say, Do you love him? Isn't that the only question? If it isn't asked, does that mean we both suspect that the answer is, No . . . ?

## IT'S THE CHEROOT

It's the cheroot, he said, tapping it with the scarlet painted nail of his middle finger, it's the cheroot that will solve the mystery. We looked at this smoked-down stump, soggy in its plastic bag. Not this, he said, this is a cigar, true Havana; I am talking about a cheroot. He stood up and walked away. His short swingy red jacket showed off his small waist, his slender hips rolled very neatly as he walked in his brief skirt and stiletto heels. He turned as he reached the end of the wharf and flashed a smile, the whiteness of his teeth dazzling in his plum-dark face.

Not your problem, he said, and walked up the steps to the boat, his heels clicking on their wooden planks, the muscles of his calves made round and taut by the highness of the heels, and stood in the prow while it cast off and headed down the river. We watched the old steam launch lumbering through the oily swell. No, it was not our problem. We went on with the card game; there wasn't a lot of money at stake, none of us had any to speak of, but that made the prospect of even a small amount more enticing. I picked up my newly dealt hand; the boat was nearly at the bend of the river. It blew its horn, a melancholy sound, old and patient and elemental as the river itself. My cards looked promising. I stared out at the greenish water, the greenish mangroves along the bank, the absent boat. Not our problem. She was young, and pretty enough; she should have had a life. I concertinaed the cards in my hand. The death of one diminishes us all. The beautiful young man with his clue or perhaps it was a warning of the cheroot might not have said that, but that is how he would act.

The Lizard lost as usual. He mooched off down the wharf. Spangle as usual won. He picked up the small pile of coins and slid them into his pocket. Every week we played cards, and it seemed as though Spangle always won. Was he a better player? I didn't think so. But luck was with him and that was all that counted. He had a pretty wife, too. He took his winnings home and gave them to her. Maybe that was what protected his luck. I went and stood beside the Lizard, where he leaned on a post, gloomily staring at the greenish water heaving itself around the piles of the wharf. Even the water is tired, in this place. I imagined I could see a shimmer at the bend of the river where the launch had disappeared. It won't be back for another week. No one much wants to come here. And nobody seems any good at leaving.

Sometimes I imagined the Lizard bending over and just sliding into the water, like some scaly amphibian. Except of course he wasn't, did not even look like one, not like his namesake even. The water was deep here, and like most of the people who lived along the river he couldn't swim. The water did not make you want to get into it for any reasons of pleasure.

Suddenly he said, with surprising vehemence: How can she work, like that? It's not natural, I don't see how she can do it.

After a minute I guessed him to be talking about Andrea. Like the rest of the people here he thinks she is a woman. You mean the heels, I said. It's a skill they have, women.

Still seems funny, for a police, said the Lizard.

Plain clothes, I said, and he laughed.

Spangle's wife came up the track. She was wearing high-heeled sandals, with skimpy shorts and a shirt tied at the waist. Her skin is very brown, we're all burnt by the sun here, but hers is somehow natural looking, as though she'd have been born like that, and her eyes are enormous and dark with bluish whites. She took little steps, sort of mincing, that's what the high heels did. See, I said, they just can.

She paused by the store, which in this place is pub, and café, post office, grocery, you name it, if it is to be bought it has to be bought here. There's a sign across the front, painted by Slide, the fat man who owns it. Emporium of Broken Dreams, it says, in dripping red letters on an old piece of timber. I heard

Spangle's wife say once how she thought it sounded like a poem.

Slide's boy was carrying in the boxes the launch had unloaded on to the end of the wharf. A lot of grog. Tins of food. It's grim if the stores run out, and I'll say this for Slide, things might run down but so far they don't usually run out. You might end up eating hearts of palm out of a can when what you wanted was baked beans, but at least it's food.

I once asked Slide, How come hearts of palm? He replied: Why not? There are a lot of things in the world, Ken.

The opium doesn't run out. So far it hasn't, and everybody has faith that it never will. Nobody ever questions its just always being there. Maybe they're superstitious; better just to go on having faith. Maybe things would be better if it did, I said to Slide once. He laughed at me. After everyone had killed each other, you mean?

Andrea never notices the opium. Well, I suppose he notices, just pretends he doesn't. The fact is the place runs smoothly. Well, until the girl was murdered. It'd be good to think that it was some passer-by but we never have those. No tourists come here. The boat is the only way in. Occasionally somebody who may be official but they don't stay, they leave on the same boat. It comes in, unloads the stores, takes the venom and goes again.

The Lizard has a tent, quite a fancy affair with its own veranda. Spangle and his wife live in one of the shacks; Slide has the best of them. The fisherman's is okay. There's a guy called Tarantin who lives round the bend of the track with his old mother. The Chinese have a kind of compound of huts and lean-tos and canvas shelters; I am never sure how many of them there are. Sometimes I squint at it, when the sun is glinting off the flattened paraffin tins that form their roofs, and see a fabulous palace of many pavilions, but that's hard work even for my imagination.

That's about it, except for a couple of old-timers further down the river. And the hippies that live by the creek, further inland. Creek; more of a swamp. There are kids all over bites but they don't seem to notice. And of course me; I was lucky there was a shack, more tumbledown even than most, but it was vacant. It belongs to Slide; I expect everything does. He put a tarp over the roof so it's fairly watertight.

Slide's store is closed by a wooden shutter that folds down to the counter and has a huge padlock, that he never clicks home, and even when the shutter is down it doesn't necessarily mean that the shop is shut. On the evening of Andrea's visit he beckoned me over, and put a bottle of his whisky on one of the rickety tables on what he calls the terrace. I know if I sit with Slide often and long enough I'll learn all there is to know about this place. Slide's okay to talk to, the others are hopeless, you have to play cards. When you drink with Slide you know he's totting it up, it'll end on the slate with all your other purchases. Only yours, he doesn't expect you to pay for his.

Sometimes the whisky is some terrible moonshine that comes from a still somewhere off in the mangroves. Tonight it's half-way decent, not Scotch of course but some okay colonial imitation. The stomachs are strong here. I sometimes think that Slide likes me, and that's probably why the others accept me. We all look the same, me, Slide, the Lizard, the fisherman, Slide calls him the Fisher King but I've never thought he was that good at his job. If we depended on his fish to feed us we'd get pretty hungry. We're all burnt mahogany by the sun, our eyes a bit watery, dressed in singlets and shorts and thongs, our bodies worn and sinewy. Even Spangle, who's probably the youngest, looks a scrawny old bird.

The dead girl is the daughter of the fisherman. If he's the fisher king does that make her the fisher princess? She used to flit, down to the shop, along the edge of the river, a thin and child-shaped little woman with a great red frizz of bushy hair on her head and a poignant little face. She wore dresses like nightgowns and it's as well she didn't go out after dark or you'd have taken her for a ghost. I thought of her as I took a pull of the whisky, a kind of memorial toast. Wondered if maybe now her figure would flit through the dark nights of the river, really a ghost. I wished her spirit rest. I suppose you can't expect that until her murderer is caught.

Know what a cheroot is? said Slide. He pumped the paraffin lamp and lit it, casting a yellow gloom over the tables, the beaten earth of the terrace, the single tree that leaned over his yard. The whisky looked very brown in the glasses. I read somewhere that whisky in its natural form is colourless, that the brown is caramel. I suppose it's to make you think of peat and amber-coloured mountain becks. I often think of words like beck, and brook, when I look at this oily river and its sluggish creeks. But we can't choose the words we live with.

You smoke it, I said, it's like a cigar.

It comes from India, he said. It's open at both ends. Originally from India. Could be anywhere now.

Andrea said it would solve the mystery.

Andrea will solve the mystery. He's a clever girl.

I nodded. So Slide knew about Andrea.

Not least because he isn't a girl, said Slide, and no one twigs. You know, he said, his mother called him that. Apparently there's some Italian painter of that name. She looked at books of beautiful pictures before he was born; supposed to give her beautiful thoughts and so she'd have a beautiful baby. It's a bloke's name there, apparently.

Slide looks sceptical at the best of times, and now even more so. You have to wonder, he said. Maybe in Italy, but not here. It could have an effect.

Why doesn't anyone else know?

They don't know much, Ken. Better like that.

I suppose he is quite beautiful.

True.

Slide took out a packet, a yellow box with some pattern in red and gold. He opened the lid and slid back cellophane. Cheroot? he said.

Where did you get these?

I've got a lot of things in there.

He lit it for me. It was quite coarse, but it didn't taste stale, as it might have done, I thought, something Slide had had forever. Do you sell a lot of these?

Not a lot, no.

I said if I sat drinking with Slide I'd eventually find out what there is to know about this place. But I should also have said that it could take a very long time.

Cheroot's a French word, he said. They got the word from India, too.

Slide's got three books in the store, has had for a long time, I reckon. The same three. But you often see him sitting on his terrace, reading. Not one of the three. I suppose that's where he gets to know about cheroots and such.

Why do you stay here, Slide?

Got to live somewhere. He blew fragrant smoke into the air. Why do you, Ken?

I shrugged. I was writing my book, but I didn't want to tell people that.

One day you'll finish it, he said. Then you'll see. Whether you leave or not. Can, or want to.

So he knew that, too. I laughed. But I could feel my

cheeks getting hot. Shame-faced. I turned it towards the river, secretly flowing past the wharf. This immense burden of water, always flowing, always and never the same.

People are funny, he said. They get fond of the places they live in. Even so God-forsaken as this.

I looked along the track. The shacks were dark. Nothing to do at night, nobody reads, there's no television, they just go to bed when the light goes and get up when it comes back. The opium is not a night-time activity. Only the Chinese palace showed wavering slits of lamplight, or candle flame.

Why do we say God-forsaken, I wonder? I think God is more here than in most places I've been. What do you say, Ken? Will we find God here?

Maybe, if we look for him.

Good point.

We'd got to the stage where the conversation had become lazy. Well, lazy; our voices were, and my brain, but the subject matter was too energetic for me. The level of the whisky had dropped considerably. I wasn't sure I could afford much more. I stood up, and stretched.

To our cots, said Slide, our virtuous cots. He drained his glass and stood up too. He raised his hand, and padded with the slow gait of the fat man round to the back of his emporium, the bottle under his arm.

When I first came here I used to get up at dawn to watch the harvest, but there's not a lot to see. The snakes begin to stir in the grey morning twilight, and the men suddenly sinuous as ghosts disappear into the scrub and come out with hessian sacks with the creatures in. They keep them in boxes under the wharf, for coolness, and then just before the launch is due they milk the venom. It's a skill these people have. The money's okay, not a lot but not bad for the amount of effort involved. They'd say it was dangerous work, but they make it look easy. Not that you'd catch me trying.

Slide told me that at one time, when there were a lot more snake catchers on the river, they'd make dry ice with carbon dioxide cylinders so they could milk them straightaway and freeze the venom. But they decided they didn't need that much effort, the launch brings a sackful of the stuff and they put the newly harvested venom in that. I said to Slide that some entrepreneurial person could probably get them a much better price, organise a market that would make them a lot richer.

Entrepreneurial, said Slide, pronouncing the word in a set of small bites as though he'd never heard it before, let alone pronounced it, and wasn't sure he could manage it now. He squinted. What would be the point of that? he asked.

More money, I said.

What would be the point of that? What would they spend it on, here?

They could use it to get away.

Then they wouldn't be venom hunters. Logic, he said, logic, Ken.

I've given up getting out of bed at dawn to see the snake catchers melt away into the scrub, I've kept my old habits of late to bed and late to rise even though it means buying a lot of paraffin, but I do sometimes still watch the milking. Spangle is the best at it, the forked stick, the grasp of the head, the opening of the mouth. Tarantin's mother is the next best, she smiles so widely her teeth nearly fall out and she has a strange violent action of her arms, but she gets the job done slickly, in the end.

There seem to be certain days for the opium smoking, they happen in their own time, people know though it never seems to be discussed. I wonder where it comes from. I guess the Chinese grow it, in the hinterland somewhere, they'd be the ones you'd expect to have the skills. I don't know, and I don't ask. I don't smoke it either. I thought of what Slide said, about me not leaving. He's wrong there. I'll go, when the time's right. It isn't yet. Once he said to me, Ever think you'd like to find Xanadu? Staring into a glass. Xanadu, I said, my voice a bit husky from the drink; it was moonshine that night, I remember thinking they should colour it pale blue, as a warning. Not just a fragment, Slide went on, the whole thing. No interruptions here. It was then I realised he was talking about the Coleridge poem. I had thought about opium, what it might do for me, but there were too many warnings. No happy endings. As Slide said, the poem was only a fragment. And anyway I'm not a poet. Doesn't it take more than it gives? I said.

Maybe, replied Slide. I'd learned that conversations with Slide didn't have ends. All my time in this place, I realised, would be just the one dialogue. It was like a piece of music, with themes uttered, dropped, reiterated, not always articulated but never lost. There was never any hurry to move it along. Another day Xanadu, or opium, would come up. Afterwards I wondered if he'd had thoughts along those lines, himself. I thought I should have said, What about you? It might have been polite.

I supposed the venom hunters spent their profits on opium. The food didn't cost much. Sometimes the hippies brought in fresh vegetables that they'd grown, and fine green stems of marihuana, but people didn't have the habit of fresh much, around here. The grass was good, healthy, out of the ground, I sometimes took on a bit of that. Opium. If I took up opium I'd have to become a venom hunter.

The day after the launch left it came back again. We were sitting by the wharf, on Slide's terrace, playing cards. Spangle was winning. The launch turned the corner of the river and its melancholy horn sounded. I nearly said, How sad is the sound of the horn in the mangroves, but I thought, I'm not that silly.

I might have, to Slide. We all looked at the launch, it never comes except once a week, and for a moment I wondered if it was yesterday, if somehow the intervening events had been a moment of hallucination, and here was the launch arriving, and Andrea would step off in his high-heeled shoes and his flirty red jacket and tell us, The cheroot is the clue. But if it hadn't happened yet, how did I know it?

Andrea did step off, but today he was wearing jeans like a second skin and a silk shirt the colour of cream, with little red shoes like ballet slippers on his feet. He skipped down the steps and sat with us. Lizard said, Back already. Andrea said, Alas, and Slide came out of the Emporium, pulled a chair from the other table and sat on it, back to front. We finished the game. Slide said, Deal you in? Andrea shook his head. Nobody said, Why are you back here so soon? I suppose they knew. Slide got up, in his ponderous yet efficient manner and got a bottle of whisky. The good stuff.

Slide brought a bunch of shot glasses, spread them out and filled them, pushing them in front of us. Andrea smiled. On duty? Picking it up and taking a mouthful. Spangle shuffled the cards, neatened them, and put them on the table. The launch gave a cough of steam.

Spangle's wife came along the road from their shack, in her short shorts and tied-up shirt, her high-heeled sandals quiet on the dusty track, her long brown legs forced into small steps. She came up to the table and looked at Spangle. He didn't catch her eye. No woman has ever looked at me like that, and I don't think I would want one to. It was a naked look, raw, full of longing, love, desire, all moiling together, and with utterly no hope. She dropped her heavy dark lids over the splendid brown and bluish white of her eyes, but she couldn't hide the tremble of pain in her mouth. She bent her head so her swags of dark hair fell forward beside her face. Andrea stood up swiftly and brought a chair, placing it with a kind of gallantry at the table, filling one of the little glasses with the good whisky and placing it in front of her.

Slide filled the glasses again. Everybody drank, not tipping it down as you do with a shot glass but slowly, even contemplatively. Andrea's face was sorrowful. No venom today, he said, that can follow the usual timetable. We all sat and drank. It was like a very dull party, where there is nothing to say, except it wasn't, because there was so much tension in the air, I imagined everybody felt as strung-up as I did.

Andrea leaned back in his chair, his body an elegant curve across its round metal back. Still got those cheroots, Slide? he asked. Slide nodded. And you're still smoking them, Andrea said to Spangle. He nodded. But not you, Mrs Spangle. She shook her head. People didn't smoke much tobacco here. Their rations of opium, that seemed to do them.

Mrs Spangle. I suppose she had a name, but I didn't know it. She looked at Andrea. I'd like to put a dress on, she said. He nodded, and she walked off; we watched the taut movement of her calf muscles as she picked her small steps down the track. She came back after a while, wearing a dress of some stiff shiny material that creaked as she walked, in a bright purplish pink colour, the colour of bougainvillea, if there had been any about. It was strapless, in a boned heart shape that fitted against her chest. She wore the same sandals, and it occurred to me that she walked as though her body was shackled, that chains prevented the free long steps that her legs were made for. She carried a white plastic handbag, very shiny and cheap looking, and when she sat down she put it carefully in her lap and held it tightly between her two hands. It had an orange plastic buckle that clashed with the dress. I don't think I've ever seen a sadder object than that clumsy white plastic handbag, so big, so shiny, so ugly. Andrea put more whisky in her glass and she took a long sip.

Everybody seemed to know what was happening. Well, up to that point. I wondered that nobody needed to speak of it, but there was evidently understanding. She held the handbag tightly in one hand and undid the buckle, sliding the other hand inside the bag. She felt for a moment, and brought out a tarnished brass compact. I'd never seen her wear make-up, powder in that climate would set like mud after rain with creeks of sweat running through it. Andrea's fine plum-dark skin was never touched by it.

She put the compact on the table, and her hand back in the bag, felt around, and pulled out a snake, a small and

I knew particularly poisonous one. People took breaths and leaned back. Her other hand pushed the bag away, and with a quick movement pulled the boned top of her dress down, so her round brown breast popped up over the top of it, and in the same moment she applied the snake to it. All the men stood up, chairs fell over, and then they remained where they were, as she dropped the snake and fell back in her chair. She looked up at Spangle, that look of love, and longing, and no hope at all, then slid down into the dust. He knelt, and held her, and after a while she was dead. Not an easy death, or a pretty one, but at least Spangle held her tight through all the indignities of it. Andrea and Slide and the rest of us walked down to the end of the wharf and looked at the boat. Nobody seemed to think of trying to save her.

Of course not, said Slide. Not a hope.

Don't you have antivenene in the fridge? I asked. After all, this was a community of poison hunters. They must be prepared for accidents.

His gaze shifted to the bend in the river where the launch had disappeared, taking Andrea and the stretcher that had appeared out of its depths and carried off the shrouded body of Spangle's wife. We'd laid her on it and wrapped a worn white sheet around her, the creaking bougainvillea-coloured dress springing out as we tried to enfold it. Slide shrugged.

It bit her fingers, he said, in the bag. That would have been it, she wouldn't have needed to apply it to her breast.

Did she have a name, of her own?

Aurora.

Aurora. I wondered if anybody had ever called her that. Had Spangle? I'd never heard it, all the time I'd been here.

I wanted things spelled out. So you all knew, I said.

What?

That she'd done it.

Again he shrugged. I spoke again, mainly to myself. That she, that Aurora, murdered the girl.

I thought Slide's look meant yes. I went on: Why?

Slide still gazed at the bend in the river. Because, I said, Spangle had been on with the fisherman's daughter, and that was the clue of the cheroot. And everybody knew Andrea had come to take her away. But he didn't know she was going to kill herself.

Well, said Slide. And I suddenly thought, he is disagreeing with me. Andrea did know. That was his kindness. And why nobody ran and got antivenene.

So, I said, justice is done. Slide raised his eyebrows. I went on, softly, to myself, Aurora has paid, and Spangle is okay, except that he has lost his wife and his lover. And maybe his luck.

Ah, said Slide, you think that possibly he will lose at cards now?

# THE ORIGINAL IS UNFAITHFUL TO THE TRANSLATION

On a summer's day in a house in the Paris suburbs a young student called Susan Kaye opened a filing cabinet and took out a diary which she leafed through and looked into. The entries were sometimes in French and sometimes in English, except for the very last words, which were *Ich Liebe Margot*.

She would not have expected to be doing such a thing. She believed she was not a person who did such things. Twenty years after that summer's day in Paris, and another twenty years ago now, she had stayed alone in the flat of a friend who was famous for keeping diaries. As a form of superannuation, the friend had said, one day their gossip and anecdotes about literary people and intellectuals would be worth a lot of money. On a small wooden bookcase underneath a window was a whole row of bulging well-bound books, and Susan knew they were the famous diaries. She could have looked at them but she did not, out of respect. Even when she believed they were intended for public consumption. Because she was not a person who read other people's diaries.

But on that day forty years ago in the house in Paris she had done so. She had read *Ich Liebe Margot* and wondered why Gerard had written it in German. He was an Englishman, a French scholar, and Margot was a French woman, neat and plain in that handsome way of French women, like a small brown bird. Maybe he wanted the particular music of the German sounds. Susan did not speak German but she knew what the words meant: *I love Margot.* The French *J'aime Margot* did not have quite the same feel; maybe it was this other rich exotic foreignness that he wanted, believing that French was already a kind of mother tongue and everyday. Susan felt the words in her chest, a slight choking feeling as though they were about her.

They were written a long time ago, and Susan wondered if they were still true. They had another quality about them, as though Gerard Percy was making a speech to himself, was watching himself making this declaration and not just observing but constructing a young man in love. She wondered if Margot had ever seen them? Now there was a complicated and ramified bourgeois marriage, which Susan had often witnessed but until now only as its protagonists had shown it to her. Now she was examining it for herself, in filing cabinets and bookcases and boxes in the study, in armoires and dressers and chests of drawers, in painted china and brown cooking pots and battered aluminium saucepans. She was a research assistant, not paid really, though there was a small grant subsidising something. She had decided that research in a foreign language should not be confined to the words on the page.

She knew that Margot was really Marguerite, that the diminutive was a family nickname. She knew that they always spoke French together and that their five children were expected to speak this language. Mostly they lived in Cambridge; that was where Susan had worked with him. He was making a translation of Rimbaud, a scholarly activity, not aiming to turn out English poems which would catch the originals in some way but offering the French on the left-hand side of the page and an English translation on the other, discussing possible meanings in academic prose. Susan would have liked to try writing English poems which would somehow *be* Rimbaud, but Gerard was shocked by that; the French was the poems. You must know, he said, the conflation *traditore/traduttore*? Susan was a bit offended; who could study a foreign language without knowing that? It means translator/traitor, she said. Indeed, said Gerard: *Traduire c'est trahir*. To translate is to betray, said Susan. Excellent, replied Gerard. As you observe, not quite so neat in French. And in English not neat at all. We need the Italian for the sharpness of the connection. So, he went on, our Rimbaud; we will have as little betrayal as humanly possible. He made it very clear that the English was to be a handmaidenly tool.

Like herself, thought Susan. She had a simple name but did not wish to be a simple person. A scholar she had plans to be, but not therefore a sexless woman devoted only to the mind. She aimed to speak French like a native of the country, and longed to be mistaken for one. The nearest she'd got was a man in a train asking her did she come from Belgium, which was a start. Gerard did not ever sound like a French person, he spoke beautiful complexly syntaxed eighteenth-century French with an English accent which in France was considered eccentric and charming, but which sounded odd to other English scholars of the language. One of Gerard's students told her it was what grand Englishmen used to do, speak perfect French but always with English vowels and consonants. It was a way of keeping the frogs in their place. Gerard called up and down the staircases of the tall regency house in Cambridge in this strange hybrid, and Margot answered.

The armoire in the Paris house was full of wedding linen. Sheets embroidered white on white, with garlands and violets and ears of wheat. Pillowslips fastened with tiny pearl buttons. Immense piles of tea towels of heavy linen huckaback with a fine red stripe, monogrammed in red with the initials of Margot's name as a young girl, her *nom de jeune fille*; Susan liked the fact that virginity didn't come into it, as in the term maiden name. Some of the tea towels were quite discoloured with use and in all of them the linen had a slight greyish cast. She needed to examine the cupboards because she would be housekeeping here for a while on her own. Margot had given her instructions to walk down into the valley and up the hill to the next village and collect the laundry. She took a big basket and set off. At the laundry she asked for the linen of madame Percy—she thought it was clever of Gerard, that both his names were bilingual—and the woman had said in that singing way that always charmed her and which she tried to develop in her own speech, *Ah, la dame Anglaise*. Susan had said, Oh no, she is French, but the laundry woman had insisted, *Ah non, madame Percy, la dame Anglaise*, in a reproachful manner, and Susan suddenly heard Margot's voice calling up and down the regency stairs, and realised that she too spoke lovely formal French but with an English accent. She felt sad, as if Gerard had in some way destroyed his wife's heritage, so that her countrywoman thought she was an English lady.

He had taken Margot and the children to her family in Burgundy for part of the summer holiday, and would come back shortly and he and Susan would work on the Rimbaud together. It had to be finished before the autumn term started. She put the sheets and pillowcases and tea towels neatly on the lace-lined shelves of the armoire. There were cotton sacks of lavender to scent them. It was very satisfactory seeing piles of ordered linen, the plates and cups in the dresser, the ornate silver cutlery, the curious *batterie de cuisine*. The ancient housewifely satisfactions. Not to mention arcane knowledge. There were strange metal picks, rather like rudimentary forks;

Margot had told her they were for eating lobster, getting the meat out of the claws, Gerard was very fond of lobster, she always got them for him in the season, there was a special market in Paris, she took the train in. There was a flat fine metal sieve and an object rather like the wooden mushroom Susan's mother had used for darning socks; it had the same name, it was *un champignon*, and you used it to push cooked vegetables through the sieve to make creamed soups. Do you do that? she asked. Oh yes, of course, said Margot, Gerard is very partial to creamed soups.

Susan wondered if Gerard would expect her to be his handmaiden while Margot wasn't there. To run the same high bourgeois household. To shine the floors with the immemorial dance of the polishing cloth: spread it with thick wax, dance it backwards and forwards with quick jumping steps like a polka to coat the old wood, and then again with a plain cloth to polish it in, polish it up. Ah, but she was there to help with the translations; running the household was a full-time job.

Did Gerard ever say, these days, *Ich Liebe Margot*? Did he murmur, *Margot, je t'aime*? Say Margot, I love you? Or did she as well as he simply assume those words upon which this whole edifice was built?

Gerard was a big man, lean and handsome, with a fine bushy head of dark hair; Margot the little brown bird, smooth-feathered and deft, took his arm when they went out, always on foot; they didn't have a car, they walked to railway stations, and her polished little shoes moved fast to keep up with his long strides; he looked down at her with his proud smile. The proudness not specially for her but of himself. His eyes sparkled, sometimes with anger, sometimes at the comedy of things; he was good at observing folly, and finding a pointed phrase to skewer it.

Susan was tall, and took long strides too, she had long pale hair which hung down her back in the fashion of that time, sometimes held back with a band to keep it out of the books. She was golden skinned and when people heard she was Australian they said Ah, as though that explained her looks, though they also said, but you don't sound Australian. Yes I do, she replied, my accent is a perfectly ordinary educated Australian accent. She had studied French under an old mentor of Gerard's, which was how she came to be here.

Gerard sent her a postcard, announcing when he would be back, and the time of the train to expect him on. He had a thrifty dislike of the telephone. On a shelf in the study, here and in the Cambridge house, was a set of postal scales and a booklet of prices, so Margot could weigh up the scholarly mail and put the right stamps on it. Gerard did not have a lot of faith in the post office's calculations. Susan went to the market and bought some things to eat; when she thought about it she could form no picture of Gerard cooking. And that turned out to be the case. He made suggestions for possible meals, and praised her, saying she was coming on well, she had the makings of an excellent cook. He opened wine, and they had two glasses each for dinner. They worked in the mornings, then ate the sandwiches she had prepared; after lunch he had a small nap—he had been up since very early in the morning, it was before breakfast that he got his reading of fiction done—and then a walk, then more work, dinner, and again reading, scholarly this time. Susan had never led so orderly a life. She was used to working hard, but just as it happened, not in a strict pattern.

How old are you, Susan? he asked her once.

Twenty-two.

Ah. *Une jeune fille en fleurs*.

She knew that was a reference to Proust. She wondered how to put it in English. Blooming? No. In flower? A flowering young woman? None worked as well as the French.

Do you feel homesick here in France?

Not really, she said. I know I'm so lucky; Paris, living here, it's my dream. Home can wait.

Is there *un petit ami*?

No, she said. No one special.

She thought of the boys she'd known. They seemed very young and very far away from the person she was now. Even Mark whom she'd had a longish love affair with, even thought of marrying, was hard to remember clearly. The boys in Australia seemed like puppies playing on a lawn, endearing but not serious. Not till much later did she realise they were probably the same age Gerard had been when he met Margot.

She didn't know if she seduced him. Her hair fell across the page; he stroked it. Your medieval hair, he said. (She knew he would spell it like that, it was the Cambridge way.) She had the same choking feel in her chest as from the words of love at the end of the diary. After dinner she washed her hair in the several inches of water it took so long to gather in the immense old bathtub, and sat in the warm twilight evening of the garden, spreading it out with her hands to dry. He came to her bed where she was reading by the light of a dim yellow lamp, homemade from an old brass candlestick. Will you permit me, he said, in a curious formal manner, and she smiled and turned back the covers to invite him in.

He was considerate, he used what he called an English overcoat.

An English overcoat?

*Une capote Anglaise*. A French letter. Each language blaming the other for the unmentionable.

After that he came every night. He never said I love you, in any language, though he did offer endearments, in French, and odd scraps of poems some of which she recognised: Mallarmé, Baudelaire, Verlaine; the Symbolistes were his period. He called her *ma belle Suzanne*. She thought I am the mistress, of the man and the house. She wondered if she would want this to go on, to take possession of it all for herself, to become the wife as well as the mistress. Take what was Margot's and make it her own. Women did this, sometimes, these days, it was the beginning of the time when it became common for men to leave one wife and family and begin over again with another, mainly because they could, and not because the old life was unbearable.

Do you keep a diary, she asked, I mean, now? Of course, he said. The unexamined life is not worth living, don't you agree?

She wondered where he kept it. She hadn't found any married ones in the filing cabinet. The current one must be in his satchel.

There was a sale of historical papers at an auction house on the Quai d'Orsay; one of them was a letter from Rimbaud, and Gerard sent her in to look at it. He couldn't afford to buy it, but he wanted her to do as Margot did, go to the preview and read it, memorise it, and write it down for him. He already had quite a collection garnered by this means, no use for publishing but handy for research. She didn't do a good job; she thought she had remembered it but when she came to write it down, in a café round the corner, she found she hadn't, properly, there were gaps which spoiled its sense. He sighed when he looked at it. I need practice, she said. Memorisation is not a skill of your generation, he said.

On that occasion she'd bought a handsome bound volume in a paper shop in the boulevard St Michel to keep a diary in but found she needed practice at that too. She wrote down *Ich Liebe* . . . but did not know what to put after that. She folded the page over and there was a fresh one. She could not write, Tonight Gerard made love to me, not in any language she knew. She noted the names of the poems they translated and what they had for dinner.

He never stayed all night, always went back to his own bed. Hers was one of those very wide single beds, or a narrow double one, good for a passionate couple but not useful for sleeping. When he left she stirred and stretched and hugged herself with her own arms, feeling beautiful and loved and grown-up.

This went on for some weeks, then Margot telephoned; her parents would put her and three of the children on the train from Burgundy, the others staying behind with their grandparents, and Gerard would meet her in Paris and bring her back from there. He came to Susan's bed and said, Our last time. He called her, *ma traduce et trésoré*, which he said was out of a medieval poem in three languages, Latin, French and English. This is the first verse, he said:

*Ma traduce et trésoré*
*Nicht and day for love of thee*
*Suspiro.*

She did not like to ask him what *traduce* meant in the context, it is difficult to say to a lover, what exactly does that word mean? She never did manage to find out and in fact quite shortly supposed that she must have been mistaken in what he said. She looked it up in *Harrap's French/English Dictionary* and in the *Robert French* and the *Complete Oxford* but they were no help. The word *traduce* in any kind of loving meaning did not seem to exist, but still sometimes the phrase echoed in her head. Looking back, she thought how passive she seemed, lying in bed waiting for the desired man to come, dreamily making love; nights of elegant verbal passion followed by days of poetry that she was obliged to analyse and codify, catching its imagination in a strict net of academic prose. In the daytime he would make little barbed corrections, smiling to soothe the sting, and then at night he would take pleasure in her body. My medieval girl, he'd called her, and she thought now from the vantage point of her own years past of marriages, two, and children, three, that she had been like a maiden in a tower waiting for her fate and evidently Gerard had not been it, or anyway she hadn't made him be it. And that she'd known what she was doing.

The summer passed. The children sat impeccably at meals and made conversation in French, and disappeared between times to play in the garden or down by the pond in the valley. Sometimes Margot took them on excursions into Paris, and once they shut themselves in the attic for some days and then invited everybody to the performance of a play they had written, at which they sold Gerard's superior Spanish sherry to the audience for six centimes a glass. There never was lobster though she supposed it wasn't the season, and not much in the way of cream soups pressed through the fine sieve with the wooden mushroom, but the red monogrammed tea towels got plenty of use. Never by Gerard of course, not with two handmaidens in the house. The night before she left she crept down to the armoire and took one. She kept it carefully, using it only to wrap bread; it was one that had hardly been used and stayed pristine. She looked at its red embroidered monogram and remembered her handmaiden days.

At the end of the summer she worked as an assistant teacher in high school in Orleans for the autumn term. She went back to Australia in February for the beginning of the academic year to take up her PhD scholarship. The book on Rimbaud came out and was a great success in its own circles and probably the reason why Gerard Percy soon after got his chair. Its brief introductory essay was considered a masterly piece of criticism and the translations were described as conveying every possible nuance of meaning. They say that to translate is to betray, said one review, but in this case there is total fidelity. To everything but the poetry, Susan thought, as she had at the time they were doing them. Poetry is what is lost in translation, she discovered Robert Frost saying, years later.

She'd thought Gerard might send her a copy but she had to order one herself from Blackwell's. She did not think she had expected her name to be on the title page, exactly, but she had supposed it might be somewhere noticeable, if not prominent.

She had done a lot of the work on those translations. Finally she found herself in a list of names at the back, including typists and friends and dear readers and a whole lot of unknown people. The book was dedicated to his beloved wife Margot.

Well, Gerard is dead, and so is Margot. The house in the Paris suburbs has been sold, the five children are scattered. Forty years on Susan recalls reading that formal asseveration of love in a diary, and tries to remember what that summer of translation and treachery was like. For she has decided that Gerard betrayed both *la belle Suzanne* and the beloved Margot—not least by schooling her in English French—though she does not wish that she had not let him do it. A necessary treachery, she says to herself. She wonders if Margot knew, if it was his habit to bed the pretty student help, and thinks that perhaps Margot considered that was appropriate behaviour for the great man, a kind of *droit de seigneur. Droit de professeur*. She turns over in bed and cuddles up against the back of her second husband. She divorced the first for Gerard's kind of behaviour.

The title of this story is from a remark of J.L. Borges, *El original es infiel a la traducción*. He was referring to Henley's translation of Beckford's *Vathek*.

## POLYHYMNIA

Not far from here is a secret valley where the sun always shines, though it rains quite often too, so it is lush and flourishing. Its floor is a thick lawn of grass, cropped green and fine and smooth by kangaroos. It's surrounded by trees, which are not only tall but have long trunks before the branches start, so you have to look up to see them enlaced against the sky. The slopes of the valley grow fruit trees, peaches especially, the rosy yellow kind, nectarines, avocadoes, oranges and mandarins, apples, and medlars which are not ripe until they begin to rot.

There is a creek winding and falling over rocks, and large standard rose bushes, whose arched canes drop petals on the grass all summer, scenting the air with their dizzy sweetness.

In the early morning the sun rising shines horizontal between the trunks of the trees and fills the scoop of the lawn with thick golden light like pollen. The body of the young woman walking through it hazes and dazzles in the refracting glorious particles of it. Every morning, through this palpable dense sunlight, walks the young woman naked, and now in this suddenly not-so-secret valley the young man watching her cannot descry whether the yellow light shines on her or from her.

She is not tall but not short and her body is sumptuous, her flesh dense as the sun's light and as full of curves and colours as the peaches on her trees. The man supposes: as full of juices and scents and flavours too. Her hair is a bright orange colour, standing up in curling points all over her head, which seems to be covered with small dancing flames. He watches her as she walks through the tree-pillared grove, and listens to her singing:

*I come to the garden alone*
*While the dew is still on the roses*
*And the voice I hear*
*Falling on my ear*
*The Son of God discloses*
*And He walks with me*
*And He talks with me*
*And He tells me I am his own*
*And the joy we share*
*As we tarry there*
*None other has ever known.*

He smiles at the naked human eroticism of these words. It's the old story: she thinks she is singing songs of devotion to God but in fact it is human lust and longing that she celebrates. It is the song of the spinster, who thinks she is loving God but is needing a man. He has known such women, and always their ignorant virgin innocence hides from them what they are really doing. Though they are usually a good deal plainer than this girl.

As she sings she touches her body with delicate elaborate caresses, as he would were he to get his hands on it.

He steps into the pillared space. That's a powerful song, he says.

Hello, she says, isn't it. I know many more like it.

*Jesu lover of my soul*
*Let me to thy bosom fly . . .*

Her body is like an instrument producing the music of her voice. A cello, he thinks, the shape, her rosy golden colour, her tautness, the craft and the soul of her.

I could teach you other songs, he says.

Could you? Her laugh is a kind of song, too.

Of human love. Songs of the body.

Do you want to have sex with me? she asks, and comes close and puts her arms around him.

He knows he's a good lover but she astonishes him. His body says, I have died and gone to Paradise and she is one of its houris. Afterwards she brings peaches and a jug of water from the creek and they sit facing one another on the creased rose petals. She sits cross-legged, knees wide apart, so he can see her fanny, more intricately petalled than the roses she sits on. She isn't shy, but not bold either. She just is. The juice of the peaches runs down her breasts and he licks it off and they start again.

I must get on, she says, so much to do. And walks across the grass:

*He's the lily of the valley, the bright and morning star*
*He's the fairest of ten thousand to my soul . . .*

She dances with triumphant steps and her lovely peach of a bottom swaying to the exultant music that she's singing at the top of her voice.

*He will never never leave me. Nor yet forsake me here . . .*

Can you say as much? She laughs at him, over her shoulder.

*A wall of fire about me, I've nothing now to fear,*
*From His manna He my hungry soul shall fill.*

It's the sun, he tells himself, it's the sun shining through the valley, it isn't a wall of fire, and her head is not a nest of flames. Its fiery points are cool and silky soft.

*Then sweeping up to glory to see His blessed face*
*Where the rivers of delight shall ever roll.*

The rivers of delight . . . every day the man comes, and every day she dazzles him with the pleasures of her body. They lie on rose petals, and she feeds him peaches washed down with the ancient clarity of cold water. But still she walks away and sings her passionate hymns of love to God.

Why? he asks. You don't need that . . . that sublimation, any more. You're not some sad spinster not understanding the words she utters. Why don't you sing a love song for *us*?

She tips her head back and out comes that laugh that is a kind of rich wordless singing.

It's my career, she says. I like it. I'm good at it. You want your ordinary love poetry, you should see my sister Erato. But I have to tell you, she's a bit of a prude. Her stuff's good, but she doesn't live up to it. And that mountain she lives on is so damn cold.

She leans over so her breasts brush his face and kisses him. Must get on, she says. This Christian music's my favourite. Though some of the Jewish ones are nice. The old sun chants were good, too, but there's no real call for them any more.

And she walks through the polleny rose-scented light, singing . . .

*And I am left alone with Thee;*
*With Thee all night I mean to stay*
*And wrestle till the break of day.*

She grins back over her shoulder at him. Erato, she says, who needs her when you can have Polyhymnia?

## THE TRAIN CROSSED A BRIDGE

The train crossed a bridge, and for that space of time the sound of its passage clanged on the metal and reverberated in the emptiness of the road beneath. Then it was back to its normal soft clicking sounds as it rushed past the pine trees and the great bulky buildings of the industrial area, and slid swift and slowing into the station, exactly on time.

She stood by the blackboard with its notice that the train would be thirteen minutes late. The waiting room was full of people: young women with small children, and middle-aged couples. These latter were the parents of the even younger people, students, schoolchildren, who came bursting through the doors. More slowly stepped the old people, the grandparents of the small children, met by their daughters with hugs and proud presentations of the progeny. Some solitary young men and women with backpacks walked straight through the front doors into the bus that waited grumbling noise and diesel fumes right outside. Not one person in a suit. Not like the stern-faced men striding off aeroplanes. These were ordinary people, paying for themselves. She wondered if he would wear a suit. Not likely. He had sent her a picture of himself, in a denim shirt, smiling his white teeth in a jutting jaw. Would you sit on my face, he had asked her. I would like that.

Even quite decrepit people with walking frames had made their way through the doors. She wondered if he were waiting until last. Perhaps he had missed the train. He was a person who normally travelled by air, he said, so he would like to take the train, for the adventure. People said the journey through the gorge was spectacular. She was sure she would recognise him. There was the photo, and he'd said he would carry violets. She imagined a man walking out carrying a bunch of violets aloft, like the Parthenon guides holding up furled idiosyncratic umbrellas as markers for their clients.

She stood looking polished and fresh, her hair newly washed and blow-dried into a simple smart bob, like a woman of the thirties, though her clothes did not match this. She smelled of Christian Dior Dune. She was wearing neat fitting boots of polished brown leather which she knew he would admire. Beside her feet was a carpet bag, made of an old piece of kelim, pink and a pale worn green and a soft mole colour. A thoughtful person looking at it could wonder what feet had walked upon it, in what places, at what times in history, before it ended up as a bag at the feet of a woman waiting in a railway station. Her skirt and jumper were a pale caramel colour and her overcoat was chocolate brown. Though she was dressed in the colours of food, edible wasn't a word that came to mind; she was too polished and self-contained. She wore tight leather gloves in the same mole shade as the bag and a rose-pink scarf wound round her neck. Outside it was dark and cold, and away from the smelly emanations of cars and the bus the air was frostily sweet.

On her computer at home she had a folder with a large collection of letters from him, and in her head the memory of a great many late night phone calls. She always thought of his emails as letters, because they were elegantly written. Her name was Jeanie and his was Pete, and the letters were from Pete to Jeanie and the same back again, but they were about people called Pierre and Tilda. Pierre and Tilda were Pete and Jeanie in letter writing mode. Pierre would ask questions about Tilda. What sort of wine did she like? What movies had she seen? What had she eaten for dinner? What books was she reading? What did Tilda wear in bed? Black silk pyjamas? Pierre would take great pleasure in picturing that.

This was what all the letters were about: Tilda and what she thought, what she did, how she felt. Jeanie sat at the computer and wrote back narratives of Tilda. She didn't invent them, she identified them, selected and explained, but she was aware that Tilda wasn't Jeanie exactly, she was at least a kind of alter ego. She was a person Jeanie was sometimes, a person Jeanie might have liked to have been, a person that Jeanie might one day become, especially if Pierre had anything to do with it. Pete wrote back to her and his words about Tilda were so tender, so full of subtle nuance, so delicate, that Jeanie felt a kind of envy for this woman who was so appreciated, so understood. Pierre made love to Tilda in Pete's words, and that, Tilda thought, is what women want, to be made love to in words. It isn't the only thing they want, but it is a very big thing, especially when words are all there is. Words through space, in emails and telephone calls, so cleverly electronically delivered. While the people uttering them are hundreds of kilometres apart.

Then Pete started to say that Pierre and Tilda should get together. Jeanie wasn't sure. Pete on the telephone talked to Jeanie about it. He told her in quite a delicate way that he seemed to be impotent, but that he was sure this condition would not remain once there was a meeting. He described the loving things he would like to do. That was when he said he would like her to sit on his face. She demurred; not about the sitting, she said nothing about that, but about meeting; why change things when they worked so well? But Pete was determined, and so here he was. And Jeanie had dressed Tilda with care, had perfumed and adorned her, and was standing in all her cold winter splendour by the chalked blackboard advising the train's lateness. Wondering if in fact he had cried off, no, not that, that suggested communication, perhaps he had simply failed to come, and she would be left in this isolated railway station with all the taxis gone and nothing happening until tomorrow midday. She stood with her chin dipped down into her scarf, her cheeks as pink as its soft silky wool, and thought that this was probably everything finished, that Pierre would not inquire lovingly about Tilda's moods and fears, ever again. The man with the bunch of violets; maybe he was a trick, a hoax, the photograph something out of a magazine, the letters written by somebody who laughed at Jeanie's gullibility, who'd already walked through the station and seen her forlorn and waiting and was now in a warm bar chortling with an accomplice over this prime joke. Not Pete but a woman perhaps, maybe that explained their tenderness. But could a trickster feign such tenderness? Sometimes you had to have faith that honesty carried its own truth, that it was not fakable.

When he appeared the violets were in a small glass jar, one of those little mustard jars that have Grey Poupon painted on them in blue. He presented the flowers to her with a small bow. I haven't spilled a drop, he said. Perhaps this was a challenge, that she should take care not to spill any either. Not very easy in the taxi which drove very fast and then braked suddenly, over and over; on the brief trip to the motel it made her feel quite sick.

She drifted idly in the foyer while he booked in, looking sideways at him. He did not resemble his photograph at all.

The jutting jaw was not handsome but rather bulging and his hair was surprisingly black and coarse. His ears were set very low on his head and quite protuberant; above them his skull sloped to a squared-off point so he looked exactly like a Mayan pottery vessel with jug-eared handles. He had seen a picture of her; was he thinking she looked so different?

She stood near a stand of tourist brochures and looked at him out of the corners of her eyes. His body was a similar shape to his head: square shoulders and below his torso sloping down and out to a big bottom. This filled her with dismay. She was prejudiced against big-bottomed men, she thought it showed in their personalities. She felt guilty about thinking that but couldn't stop herself. She didn't much like big beer bellies either but they weren't nearly so distasteful as bulging bottoms. In the photograph he had been standing behind a kind of fountain made of a tall vase and his hands had been resting on its shoulders, interrupting the water that bubbled over the top and flowed down the sides into white pebbles on the ground beneath it. His bottom hadn't showed; she was sure she would have noticed if it had.

In the lift which seemed more creaking and decrepit than the building's age ought to have allowed he squeezed his arm round her shoulders and said, Tilda is more beautiful in the flesh than in her picture. He unlocked the door and they went into the room. No need to describe it; simply say motel, circa ten years ago, and everybody will have an image of invariable shabby sameness, the checklist of comforts considered minimal for the careful traveller, down to the print on the wall of kittens in a blue and white bowl. She set the jar of violets down on the bedside table. They seemed to have lost their smell on the train trip.

He put his black leather holdall on the table. It had a great quantity of zips as though every possible necessity must have its own pocket. From one of them he took a bottle of pinot noir. Another had a corkscrew in it. I know it should be champagne, he said, but I couldn't get it here cold. And Tilda is fond of pinot noir.

Especially if it's good, and doesn't taste of raspberry juice, she said, and he said, Oh yes, it's good. Top Yarra Valley vintage.

She took off her overcoat and hung it in the wardrobe. She didn't unpack her carpet bag, which contained a pair of black silk pyjamas, some knickers, a bra of black lace embroidered with silver ferns and a turtleneck cashmere sweater, a new packet of stay-up lace-top stockings and a sponge bag with creams and cleansers and a small bottle of Dune. It could all stay as she had neatly packed it.

There wasn't a sofa, but two vinyl tub chairs; he pushed them close together so they could sit near one another. Salut, he said, clicking his clumsy glass to hers. The wine was good. It deserves better glasses, she said. Ah, he said, Tilda shall drink out of nothing but crystal goblets.

She wasn't sure about this Tilda thing. It was so very charming in letters, so much could be said, be polished up and made poetic. But somehow Jeanie wanted to kick Tilda out of the way and say: What about Jeanie; this is me, Jeanie. But she sat and sipped and sipped at the wine and held her glass out for more. He raised his eyebrows but poured it. If he says anything, she thought, I shall say It may increase my desire which can only be a good thing but it won't take away the capacity which is very handy for me but you are the one needs to be careful. Of course she wouldn't be so rude, but she liked thinking it. Pete tried to kiss her through the wine. His teeth were very big.

She thought she should talk to him but couldn't think of anything to say. Maybe everything was already said in the beautiful letters, everything was already all used up. Was the gorge as spectacular as you hoped? she asked. Not bad, he replied. They say it is better going the other way. I wonder why, she said. Surely it is the same gorge. He said, I suppose the angle is everything.

He leaned over the arm of her chair, and smiled, with his mouth turned down and his eyes screwed up, a smile of anguish and longing and lust. You promised you'd sit on my face, he said. With your boots on, please?

Isn't it a bit soon? she said, but she knew the answer to that; at last, so long, after so many letters, so many late-night soft-voiced conversations, the idea was they would not be able to wait.

He took her hand and pulled her to her feet and over to the bed. She hadn't promised to do that. She hadn't made any response to his request at all, so she hadn't said she wouldn't either. She drank some more wine, and tried to remember Pierre's tender solicitation, the caressing rhythms of his words. Pete was unwrapping her scarf and pulling her jumper over her head. She felt herself being undressed as though she were a doll, her limbs limp, unhelping. His hands pinched her nipples through the lace of her bra. He sighed.

Bliss, he said, the word whistling through his teeth. Such bliss.

By this time she was naked except for her boots and her stockings. He lay down on the bed, his eyes screwed up, concentrated, waiting.

## IRREGULAR VERBS

The afternoon long summer Sunday and no time in it for all that's to do. The weather summer, the calendar still spring, the endless swift-passing weather of November and exams the finals the Leaving Certificate as though you couldn't just up and go all one's education just for this the gambler's turn win or lose all the future hanging on this throw of luck and skill. Studying swotting cramming, French verbs say them over rote words like a chant bring your mind to bear not the simple verb to have *j'ai tu as il a nous avons vous avez* the hard ones the tricky ones the irregular forms irregular behaviour frowned on in girls but not in verbs. Out of the house the heavy smell of roast dinner the washing up in not enough hot not enough soapy water done and dried and put away, the family making the most of the weekend the house busy dressmaking carpentry hair-curling homework. Sitting out the front in the shade at the side of the front veranda the red brick wall stuck on the cream-painted weatherboard, a corner of coolerness, no trees to sit under this is the seaside the cruel salt wind allows no trees, scrubby geraniums and the scent of stocks in the sea summer evenings is what you get, no grass either just ineradicable sticky weed flaunting its shiny green discs in the shifting sand where should be buffalo grass, not even in the front here the elephant-skinned frangipani whose deep glamorous perfume is its surrender to the moon. The beach girls go past with their ruched bloomer cossies, their little-legged streamlined one-pieces, their copious bra-and-shorts numbers, their towelling beach coats and bags of coconut oil and biscuits and lollies and cordial, giggling behind their hands skylarking or saving themselves for the boys and the beach, intent on this life and death struggle in the bitter game of mating.

The verb *s'asseoir* to sit as in sit yourself not just irregular but with its reflexive pronoun changing, *je m'assois, tu t'assois, il s'assoit* and that's the easy present tense. Wait till brain gets to the subjunctive. Of course the theory is brain knows all this already this is just revision but brain could panic no no stay calm of course it's just revision concentrate let the deep cortex do it it's all there. There's a passing child wailing where's the beach I want the beach the mother soothes just there see just there that little bit of blue by the corner we'll be there in a moment big brother walks on the road and the melted tar burns his feet he yells and dances but always has to land back on the tar again until he can get across the burning concrete gutter to the tufty sandy grass the prickly gazanias where's your thongs I told you to bring your thongs.

*Plaire* to please: *je plais je plus je plairai* I please I pleased I will please.

Mervyn next door comes home in a taxi odd he only left this morning on his annual two weeks' holiday his mother told my mother so hard to get Mervyn to go on holiday he really needs a break from his job as a wire drawer he's going to Sydney on the flyer to stay with his Auntie Dolly, but here he is back and in a taxi too. Does he dye his hair my sisters ask themselves, Grecian 2000 to hide the grey they reckon he combs it through it's so slick and shiny and dark cruel sisters you're going to marry him they say you'll be Mrs Mervyn Mrs Mervyn Jones no I won't I say but they make it happen no I won't I won't but they laugh and point and there I am Mrs Mervyn Jones keeping house in her faded cotton house dress but at least I wear a belt our mother wears a belt some women don't sloppy shapeless sloping the belt is the line between pride and not, doesn't matter what the waist is like underneath you can let the flesh go baggy but the dress without a belt is a message you don't care and you must care otherwise all is lost. Mervyn seems to have a woman in his lap small and stiff he has a bit of a struggle to get out he puts his suitcase on the grass and leans back in and takes out the woman she is made of marble he leaves the suitcase there and carries her one arm round her feet pressed into his stomach the other holding her draped bottom his head pushed sideways by her pointed marble breasts, staggering a little and careful he must not drop her, the suitcase safe from the passing cossied girls the sea is just there in a minute they will have it they do not care about a battered old cardboard port. Of course I will not marry Mervyn Mervyn is not the marrying kind Mervyn has a marble woman Mervyn is too old but when the cruel sisters sing Mrs Mervyn Jones Mrs Mervyn Jones there it is happening and I can't stop it I am living beside my own parents in a house with camellias in the garden fancy camellias so close to the sea but Mr Jones is a good gardener now he is retired from the coalmines working in his backyard his trousers tied with string around the calves.

*Pouvoir* to be allowed to have permission to be able: present *je peux* or *je puis* past historic *je pus* subjunctive *je puisse.*

There is a car a pale green Morris Minor pulling into the gutter just outside my house cars rare enough in this street let alone stopping maybe this is the man I will marry one day he will come and take me away from all this but not just yet now I am learning these verbs and he may be tall and with a sculpted brow and light brown wavy hair though I don't care about looks really what I care about is interesting men reading books and talking about them but now is not the right moment and besides I am not dressed for it in these short old shorts and a shirt so often washed you can't see the flowers printed on it any more and my hair plaited hanging down my back I look like a child not like a woman to sweep off her feet and carry away to happy ever after it is too soon for happy ever after. The car pulls out again it is disappointing there is not a handsome man coming to visit but just as well French is tomorrow my love must wait the verbs won't.

Mervyn is gone a long time I expect he is explaining to his mum what has happened to the trip on the flyer and the holiday and what about Auntie Dolly how are they going to let her know it is a Sunday no telegrams and no telephone there's the one at the corner opposite the bus stop but Auntie Dolly doesn't have one she will think he is killed or lost not to mention a marble woman how is he explaining the marble woman? I sit on my stool my mouth silently reciting the verbs Mervyn comes out and picks up the port and waves I wave back the cruel sisters always say how handsome he is what a lover whoo whoo he has got a nice craggy face and a cleft chin and big brown eyes but the hair is too long and curling and indeed it does look too dark and maybe it is Grecian 2000 just comb through and the grey disappears does it come off on your fingers I wonder I will never find out I do not care for his looks I will pummel my sisters the next time they sing Mrs Mervyn Jones why can't they be Mrs Mervyn Jones it is because I am the eldest they say.

*Vouloir* to wish to want to be willing: present *je veux* future *je voudrais* subjunctive *que je veuille* may I want. People say the subjunctive is dying out but how can it we need to express what might have been, what might still be, what could be were things to be so, or so . . .

French is all that is left the last exam all the rest are done it was westerly weather the whole week and the pages were covered with grit the wind blew it through the windows open because it was hot and we sweated in our rayon school dresses they are old and stiff and smelly the detachable white collars frayed after tomorrow we will never wear them again we have been making them last the sweat drops on the page and turns to mud with the grit I write and write because all my subjects are essays except French I have to get it all down and arrive at the end of the argument I have constructed and then at the end everybody comes out and says how terrible they were they are sure they have failed and most of us aren't being honest but this is what you have to say, it was terrible I didn't know anything what dreadful questions I know I have failed and this is a protection against the evil god of exams who would fail us for hubris if we said it was quite good I got the questions I wanted and I think I managed to get reasonably good answers down, I was especially pleased with that last essay. Can you imagine it it would never happen, we lay our tribute of sorrow and fear at the feet of the god of exams and maybe he will smile upon us. There is a faint breath of air from the south maybe this is the beginning of a southerly maybe it will be cool for French coolish anyway.

*Vaincre* to conquer: *je vaincrai je vaincs je vanquais* I will conquer I am conquering I conquered.

There's the click of the front gate the iron latch thunking softly as it is lifted back and the sound repeated when the gate is shut and the latch put back into place the gate itself doesn't squeak our father has just oiled it so it is smooth he likes the place to run smoothly and I stand up to see who it is just peering round the corner of the wall and as I expected it is my cousin who often comes on a Sunday afternoon to visit we like to see her but our mother does get a bit irritated because she doesn't know whether Janet will come or not I don't mind she says I would just like to know beforehand but it is quite fun it makes a change having a visitor and she is a help she taught me to use the treadle sewing machine my mother tried and couldn't and Janet noticed that I wasn't coordinating the pedalling with the turning of the wheel on the machine and when that was fixed there I was and sewing myself clothes. Janet is a lot older than me and very large like the women in my father's family and pretty fat with it she thinks I am like her big and fat and a woman men don't look at and maybe she is right but I think I am more like my mother's family who are neat and slender but she worries me I look at myself and think I must be like her or she wouldn't see me like that. I say hello and wave the book of French verbs and she nods and goes inside. She'll talk to my mother she'll have brought some work knitting or embroidery my mother will have to stop what she is doing and sit and do some handiwork too and then she will make a cup of tea and lucky she did some baking there is a coconut raspberry slice to eat with it she usually bakes for the weekend a good housewife always has something homemade to feed her family. After a bit father will come in from the garden and have a cold shower in the laundry in the backyard once I looked through the crack in the stable door and saw him standing there naked with his round poking out tummy and his penis I hadn't seen a penis before except on babies of course but it did not look in any way surprising but I felt unworthy looking at someone who didn't know I was looking so I straightaway stopped and didn't do it again it's a cold shower in the laundry in winter he has to have a warm bath and then he will play the piano and Janet will sing she didn't think she could but he has been patiently teaching her and now she sounds good a rich contralto voice and here she is her voice pours through the open windows of the front veranda singing *Now sleeps the crimson petal now the white* and I am filled with longing and the sadness of wanting *Now folds the lily all her sweetness up* it is so beautiful you want it and you are filled with desire for the wanting and you love it and can't bear it *Ah fold thyself my dearest dear and slip into my bosom and be lost be lost in me.* And I am sweet sixteen and never been kissed so my father says and it is true and maybe it always will be nobody ever will kiss me and there will be never anybody wanting me to slip into his bosom and be lost in him my aunts think I am a bluestocking girl and will never be married. Wanting to go to university is no way to get a husband and as for this French business what's she learning French for nobody speaks it only the French over there not here what good's French to her shorthand and typing that's what's useful leave school at fifteen do a business course and get a nice steady job you might even get to be secretary to the boss if you are a good girl and who knows where that might lead not that you would have expectations just a nice steady job and save money and put together a glory box lay-by things a girl needs six pairs of sheets to be properly married not that any of that including being the boss's secretary is doing Janet any good. Once I was a brown beach girl every year forgetting and burning myself lobster red each summer's beginning and peeling in agony for several days and then I was set up, tanned and comfortable for the endless days in the water. But now it is French verbs.

Janet told us a story about a friend of hers and a man carrying this woman over a puddle she had on strappy sandals and he gallantly swept her into his arms How romantic I said and Janet said of course that sort of thing will not happen to you and me dearie we are not the sort of women men carry over puddles I did not say anything but I thought I am not sure I have given up on the idea of being carried over puddles and the like folding into bosoms and so on.

*Croire* to believe: *je crois je crus je croirai* I believe I believed I will believe.

I hear the veranda window over my head slide open. Father leans out There's a cup of tea he says I have got these French verbs to do I say Do you really he says I think you know them The exam is tomorrow I say Last minute swotting's not good he says you've worked hard all year come and have a cup of tea a bit of a relax will do you good and I think he is right of course but you never believe you know anything near as well as you might but I go inside and wash my hands and face and there are cups of tea with coconut raspberry slice and sticky orange cake, I married a good cook, says Father, as he always does, smiling his tender smile at our mother.

## AT THE POOL

I think this man in the spa is playing footsies with me. I may have inadvertently set it up because I stretched out my foot to get it near the jet and touched his leg which wasn't where I thought it would be. I pulled back straightaway but maybe he thought it was an invitation. You can't see anything in the water it is boiling and bubbling and thick with froth. When I got in I said, Ooh hot and maybe he thought this was the start of the invitation. Boiling and hot but not boiling hot, forty degrees according to the noticeboard. Hard to believe getting into the pool afterwards which seems cold you have to nerve yourself. He just looked at me when I said Hot. Who knows what spa etiquette is. Maybe you shouldn't speak to people. But you are sitting in this small pool, it's intimate, I think some kind of cool greeting is appropriate. We are human but we are islands we are bathing together but we are not friends a bit like being a diplomat really. I wonder if he is a foreigner. Maybe he is a guest of the hotel rather than a member of the gym. I should point out that this is not a sleazy kind of spa it is very serious and hard working like the pool. There are chairs about but not for lounging and there are no waiters to call for big coloured drinks with umbrellas. You get a complimentary water bottle when you join but I am not fond of the taste of plastic water. His foot is definitely brushing mine and wherever I move it to he finds me. I sit with my eyes shut the bubbling water makes a kind of meditation it takes you out of yourself and then when I open them he is hovering just in front of me. He has a big round face and a round head fringed with hair and his back and shoulders are big and round too and so I expect is his tummy but it is under the water. He looms like a whale. I wonder is there a television camera watching you could drown in this pool nobody to see you. I close my eyes again and will him to go away then open them suddenly and he lumbers off. The jets stop and since I was in last I get up and turn them on again. I ask him would he like me to do this but he just looks mournful. I see that he does have a big round tummy and red baggy shorts that puff up when the water bubbles. He is looking at me. I think he is maybe German he looks a bit Germanic, I am not keen on racial stereotypes but if they apply what can you do, he looks a bit like Goering, amiable enough but sinister too. I am not being frightened out of this spa by fishy feet brushing past, I always do ten minutes and that is what I shall do, I keep opening my eyes and he is looking at me, is it dumb yearning I see on his face, he may really be German and not speak any English and so he has to be dumb, you can't expect a woman you are playing footsie with in the spa to speak German, French now I could manage a conversation in French though I have no idea what the French word for spa could be, spa maybe, or jacuzzi, but if he was a Frenchman he would not look like this, some Frenchmen are big and round and fleshy but they have different faces they would not look dumbly at you they would manage speaking looks.

I climb out pulling the legs of my togs down as I do so, I am not one for bikini waxes and it is mostly all right but when you are climbing up steps a nose away from a fleshy staring chap who knows what can be seen. The thing about the pool is it is not the young and beautiful who use it, not generally. The gym is lean and brown and sometimes young and beautiful and sometimes ageing and raddled, there are some people I reckon must be always there because when I go at all my different times there they are, treadmilling, lifting weights, rolling round on the balls, this is their life the gym. There is a newsletter stuck on the back of the toilet door telling us useful facts like eating more fibre and personal trainers and one about thinking, it says a study of six hundred clergymen discovered that people who think regularly live longer and happier lives than people who don't, Grey Matter the topic is called, and recommends an hour's thinking a day.

I imagine all the lean gym people saying to themselves Omigod I haven't done my thinking for today oh well I'll make sure I manage it tomorrow one day off won't hurt, the way I intend to do exercise, tomorrow and tomorrow and tomorrow, I will make it up and of course you never do. But I am good at thinking, I would do hours a day some days, maybe I could hire myself out as personal thinking trainer to the beautiful lean bodies on the treadmills keep them up to the mark with their brains.

The swimmers might be more acquainted with thinking. They are almost never beautiful, are usually fat and elderly and walk gingerly on the wet pavement of the pool. Occasionally there is a goddessy body, one day a young woman with a fine slender skeleton smoothly and slightly covered with flesh, wearing a bikini made of several tiny triangles of fabric, pink and chocolate coloured and pale green in a pattern of dashes, lightly held together with little strings of fabric, it sat upon her body, did not hold it up or even cover it much it was a token that hung there and slid about and you knew that all her skin would be the same pale brown there would be no white bits and I would guess not just a bikini wax but a Brazilian I can't even bear to think about it. She swam gentle laps leaning on a small boogie board barely kicking her legs and kept jumping out to answer her mobile phone in a loud childish voice running some important business long distance. None of the rest of us has a mobile phone, or we do but we leave them in the dressing rooms. Swimming is for thinking not answering mobile phones. She had long hair and bent over in a smooth arc from her waist and brushed it down so it nearly swept the tiles and then caught it in a knot on top of her head. That day there was a man middle-aged but quite fit looking, he talked to her when she got in taking a long time the water feels cold even though it is twenty-eight degrees, he did not talk to me. Best to jump straight in he said, interrupting his laps to speak to her. When I was young I always jumped straight in, into the freezing surf at the beach, no noticeboard to tell you what temperature it had got to, I laughed rudely at people who took it slowly, much more agonising like that I said. I suppose it still is but I lack the courage or the will to jump straight in and so did the goddess even though the man so kindly recommended it.

There is nobody in today so I skip up and down water-walking the length of the pool several times. It is only fifteen metres long which is a bit of a blow, I hoped it was twenty. I always like to see the snorkelling man but he isn't here. He goes up and down with his goggles and his snorkel, his face under the water, gently breaststroking his way lap after lap he makes it look effortless. I think he is about eighty, or in his late seventies anyway, he is quite slim but you know he is old because his skin doesn't quite fit him. As though it is wearing thin and getting baggy or maybe it is the flesh inside that is wearing away and the skin like a garment too big. Every now and then he stops at the end and has a swig from his plastic water bottle, it must be thirsty work snorkelling. When I skip up and down I can see his smooth speckled back like a trout sliding through the water. Occasionally he exchanges a courteous greeting, or no, not a greeting, he offers a small comment, like sunny today, or the pool's very empty, or cold, isn't it.

I walk backwards, trailing my arms. Under the water they look like a nymph's, smooth and very white, then when I lift them out they look pinkish and a bit mottled, human again, so I keep them under the water and admire their marble smoothness. I look up and see that the German man from the spa has got out and is walking round the pool wrapped in a white towel, his red shorts hanging slack under his big round tummy. Why is he doing that? People get in and get out, move on to the next thing, we have busy lives and have to fit in that hour's thinking, this is not a pool for lounging, it is very odd to see him go and sit in one of the hard plastic chairs and just sit, wrapped in his towel. Maybe he is looking at me, watching. Sometimes a mother sits reading, once accompanying a girl with troubled legs, in my childhood we would have thought polio, but I don't think so these days, she had difficulty walking but in the pool she swam and plunged and was graceful, her mother took little notice, she was engrossed in her book, the girl could look after herself. I am graceful in the water too, skipping, turning my white arms like a dancer, swimming gentle laps, striding sideways, wafting along with my eyes closed. Every now and then opening them and the man is there, watching.

I got out. The man came up to me and said, Would you have dinner with me at the hotel tonight, in a thick awkward accent. Alas I cannot, I said, I am having dinner with my lover tonight. A small spasm of pain crossed his face. Ah, he said, hopelessly, and walked away.

No he didn't. And I didn't. I just thought this, wafting up and down the pool. I wonder does thinking this count as the proper day's exercise. Probably not, it is not exactly deep brainal activity. Wishful, it is, for I do wish that had happened, it would be nice to have a courtly invitation to dinner and to reply alas I am dining with my lover, life does not often offer an opportunity for such an utterance, of course I can say it in my head, it has a particularly rotund feel, and I can even murmur it aloud for the watching man cannot hear across the sloshing and sucking water of the pool, I am dining with my lover I say, suggesting his shape with my white arms, it is partly salt not heavy chlorine this pool and has pale blue tiles which is why my flesh looks so pale and nymph-like. I should really get a new cossie this one is twenty years old and I was thinner then there is a fair bit of bosom spilling out of these togs but at least under the water it is round and white, round being a nice word for my breasts whereas it is critical of the watching man's head and tummy and shoulders, but then the pool is frequented by saggy and ungainly people generally so a bit of flesh is all right. Occasionally there is a good-looking one like the chap the other day who came and spread his towel by the glass wall and lay sunbaking, he was brown already and lay still for a long time on his back with his arm over his eyes with only a towel between him and the hard floor, on his back like that he had a flat stomach and muscled chest, the likes of him do not look at the saggy the baggy the elderly, there are occasions you realise when the invisibility of age is a great blessing especially when you know something you suspect the young do not, that their fresh tight flesh will one day be saggy baggy and old too, it is a wonder that they don't know it but the young never do, they think everything will be different for them. But then we are all a bit odd about mortality, an old friend sent me an email the other day saying now he had only about ten years of life left probably he was much more afraid of flying than when he was young and had fifty years of life ahead of him, and I was quite shocked to think of putting a time on it like that, only about ten years left probably he said and of course that is true he is sixty-five but I was shocked that he would put it into words.

I do a lap of breaststroke, I don't swim much it makes my neck ache holding my head out of the water I should get a snorkel and goggles then I could slide through the water like snorkelling man so effortless and calm with his speckled trout back. When I stop breaststroking, watching man has gone. I look up at the clock which he is no longer sitting beneath. I have done my half hour, I can get out now.

## WE WERE SITTING IN THE GARDEN

We had been sitting in the garden drinking tea, basking in the late winter sun, but couldn't stay long. The blood and bone I had spread around the day before got too whiffy. The daffodils had finished blooming, the soaring trumpets of the King Alfreds, the tiny flowers of the tête-à-têtes, and I had cut off the dead heads and spread fertiliser around. But the pong got too much. I wasn't sorry; when I'd put it on it hadn't seemed to smell at all, and I was worried that it might have lost its potency. The stench seemed a good sign.

But then, several days later, when Moira called, I thought it would be okay to go outside again. Would you like a cup of tea? I asked. I'd rather have wine, she said. I didn't mind. Opening a wine bottle is easier than making a cup of tea, especially as I never seem able to get it strong enough for her. My father always called my tea a boy on a man's errand. Weak and helpless, he'd say. I like it like that; my tea is exactly right for me. I was surprised, though. Moira always seems more of a tea person.

I got some glasses and put the white wine in a cylindrical steel insulator. It reminds me of those brass shell cases that people used to have on their mantelpieces, for vases. They needed polishing, and I used to think, men got killed by them, women polish them. Weird souvenirs; who'd want to polish a lethal weapon, just for the house-proudness of it.

Remember those brass shell cases, I said to Moira. Yes, she said, my grandma had one; Grandfather brought it back from the war. She put roses in it. It was supposed to keep them fresh longer.

Did it?

Who knows.

We sat on curve-backed iron chairs at the pierced iron table. The sun was warm, no leaves on the trees to shade us from it. Moira took a deep draught of the wine. It's nice, she said.

I showed her the label. A New Zealand sauvignon blanc. This one was called Sibling Rivalry. The names get more outré. My son tells me we should stop drinking these New Zealand wines, they are wrecking the Australian industry. He's half New Zealander so it's all right I say. Moira was through the first glass before I'd taken a sip so I refilled. It's very good, she said. It's got a lot of flavour.

Suddenly her nose wrinkled. Toni, what's that frightful smell? she said.

Blood and bone.

No wonder it smells dead.

Has a good effect.

It's the odour of corruption.

Rubbish. It's bracing.

Not me.

Should we go inside?

Oh, doesn't matter.

I picked several heads of viburnum. Smell this, I said, it'll block out the blood and bone.

Moira sniffed. Hoo. That's heady. Decadent. It's like the plague, she said. A posy to keep the poisonous odours away.

Not poisonous at all. Blood and bone is nourishing. So we'll get flowers next year.

Next year, said Moira, with a great heaving sigh.

Something's up, I said.

Not much, said Moira. Just life as I know it.

Yeah? I said. Not meaning to be unsympathetic, but she was being melodramatic. I looked at her carefully. Moira has stayed slim; she let you know that every year on her anniversary she wore her wedding dress and it still fitted perfectly. Her face was usually smooth enough, though when the light was oblique you could see those purse marks round her mouth that play havoc with lipstick, and crow's-feet round her eyes. No way I could get into my wedding dress, if I could remember where I put it, but plumpness is a protection against wrinkles.

Today she looked somehow haggard, as though the slimness had gone suddenly bony.

She pushed her glass forward for more wine.

It's all right, I said, I've got another bottle. Expecting her to say, Good grief, no, Good grief being one of our phrases, since we had an American teacher at school who introduced us to Peanuts comics, a hundred years ago. But she said, Oh, good. I should have brought one. But my brain's not working.

Moira . . .

It's Jock, she said. He's gone.

Gone?

I'd known Jock as long as she had, of course never on the same terms. She met him when we were at uni, and there'd never been anyone else for either of them. Well, I'd always thought so.

Yes. We're getting divorced, selling the house. It's all over.

I held her hand. Now that she'd started I thought the whole story would come out, and I shouldn't interrupt.

Great moment to be selling a house, she said, and laughed a cracked ugly laugh. Pity I haven't got a pre-nup. Who had a pre-nup back last century.

Start at the beginning, I said.

Well, you know. Jock retires, I offer to, but he says no need, you're younger, you're not ready. And it's true, I haven't been back at work all that long, I'm enjoying it. I quite like the idea of pottering around on my own at home, he says, for a bit anyway. You know, the way you did when the kids were small. Well, says I, to get the full effect of that you need a baby and a toddler or two or three around, but we laughed, I was happy with the idea, I thought it might be rather nice to have a house husband. He said he liked the idea of a bit of gardening, and cooking, and he thought he might try his hand at doing some writing, why not, he had things to say. I thought this would be nice for him, because he's worked hard all his life, and I did agree that it would be good for him to have the house to himself on occasions.

We had a clanky old computer, Moira said, but he decided his retirement present to himself would be a new laptop, and he set up one of the kids' old bedrooms for a study, and said it was all going very well. Didn't want to show me what he was writing, not till he'd got somewhere, he said.

You'll say I was naïve, she said.

No, I won't, I said, and went and got the other bottle.

Maybe I should have thought, computer, internet, porn. But I didn't. I discovered it. A while ago, looking to book hotel accommodation, when I accidentally got on some trail that he'd obviously followed. I did say something, after a bit, and he said, Oh yes, research, for my novel. Novel, I said, I thought you were writing a memoir. Turned into a novel, he said. More fun. And of course, Moira said, none of this was true. He went from porn to dating sites and found this tart and that's it. He's going off with her. Nothing to be said.

What, I said. There's not nothing to be said. Not after, what is it, it's a lifetime.

Nothing useful. He's in love. He's a new man. It's a new life. He's selling the house, giving me half. He'll take the superannuation . . .

He can't do that, I interrupted. Half that super's yours.

Is it? He doesn't seem to think so. He says no point in having lawyers, they'll just take everything.

Hmm. I'm not so sure about that.

I keep thinking of the kids, their inheritance. This barracuda'll get her hands on it and that'll be the end. She'll outlive him, she's a lot younger.

He can make a will, in favour of his children.

He won't. He's besotted with her. Toni, where am I going to live? I'll never get anywhere round here for half what we get for the house, not in this market. All my life is here, my neighbours, friends. And the garden, I've worked so hard on that garden, I'm just getting it right, I love it, I can't bear to part with it.

Maybe you can buy him out . . .

Come off it. I'm going to be dirt poor as it is, I can't do a mortgage.

Maybe he'll come to his senses. I can't believe he's in his right mind, doing this.

Maybe not. But right or not, he's in it, and not likely to get out of it any time soon. He's determined to get all this done as soon as he can, so he can set up house with his lady love. Ha.

No lady, and I don't reckon she loves him. She's a barracuda. Barracudas don't love.

Moira poured more wine. The thing is, Toni, he won't even talk to me. It's as though the past has never been. Our lives together, the children, the home we made, our friends, everything, they don't exist. I think I don't exist. You know how they say it takes two to break up a marriage, and I have looked at myself, and I can't see that ours wasn't good. I often thought about it, our contentment, how well we got on, now the kids were gone and there weren't those stupid niggling arguments, and the pleasures we had, going out to films and plays, little holidays, eating meals together, opening nice bottles of wine, talking about things, okay so I suppose it wasn't mad romance, but we made love, we were a couple, we liked one another.

Can you stall, slow things down? Maybe he'll see sense.

I'm trying to. The only thing I can do is with selling the house, we've had offers but I say we can't possibly sell it so low and he is inclined to agree because he wants money to spend on the floozie but I don't know that it's going to help much longer. It's been going on for a while, you know. I didn't tell you. Maybe I thought if my friends didn't know it would go away.

That's why I haven't seen you for a bit, I said.

She nodded, her eyelids drooped. Yes. I said to myself, all the while Toni doesn't know, it's not happening.

Maybe I should talk to him, or Gilbert.

Toni and I had been friends for so long it was inevitable that our husbands were too; they liked one another, were happy to do things with the four of us. They didn't do much with just the two of them, though.

Toni looked up, then her face fell. I don't think it would help, she said.

Nothing to lose.

True. Might be horrible for you, though.

That's not a reason.

It wouldn't work. I don't think.

What do the kids think?

They're appalled. They've tried to talk to him, but he won't listen. Keeps saying it's his turn now. When hasn't it been, I ask myself.

A person came round the corner of the house, into the back garden where we were sitting. A youngish man, in a skinny tracksuit, carrying a bag. He looked at us. Surprised? I wondered. Nervous?

Ah, he said, hello, ladies. I thought I heard voices. I knocked on the front door and no one came, and then I heard voices.

I didn't believe this. Our voices had been murmuring, low, the quiet mournful tones used for death and bereavement. He would not have heard us from the front of the house.

I'm a gardener, he said. I see you have a very lovely garden here. I could help you make it even lovelier.

A gardener? Quick-witted, I thought.

Why don't I sit down with you lovely ladies and have a glass of wine and talk about it.

I don't think that's a very good idea, I said. I don't need a gardener, and we are rather busy here.

Oh? Pity.

Moira said: I think I might need a gardener. She took a card out of her handbag. Give me a ring, we can talk about it.

The man bowed, gave a kind of salute, and went off. Sloped off, I thought.

Moira! Are you mad? He's not a gardener, he's a burglar. He didn't hear us talking, he was casing the joint. He'd be a drug addict, looking for easy money, they always are, around here. You know that.

His manners are nice. And did you see his eyelashes! I adore sooty eyelashes.

No one who calls women like us lovely ladies has nice manners.

Moira poked out her bottom lip. He could be interesting, she said.

Only if you're looking for a gigolo. And I thought you said you weren't going to be rich enough for that.

We'll see. She picked up her bag. I should be going, she said.

You're not driving?

No. I walked.

Stay a bit, I said. I don't think you should go yet. Give me a minute, I haven't taken in what you said yet.

No, it needs some doing. She sat down again. I haven't got hold of it myself, and I've been trying for some time.

I held her hand again. We're such old friends, we're more used to sharpness and jokes than to commiseration, though we have comforted one another often enough in sad times.

You could come and stay here, I said.

She looked at me, I thought I detected a certain exasperation.

Not forever, I said, I don't mean permanently, but if you need time to get sorted.

Thank you, Toni, that's sweet of you. I will, if I need to.

I walked out with her to the street. The burglar was coming out of the house opposite.

All these lovely gardens, he said, and no one needs a gardener.

Or a burglar, I muttered.

Moira went up the hill, the young man down. Burglar, drug addict, axe murderer—maybe it was an axe in the bag—gardener even, I was glad she wasn't walking home with him. I watched her slowly making her way. I was thinking of safety. I'd have thought Moira's marriage about the safest I knew. I thought, it is true, we are never safe.

I went inside to Gilbert. Do you want the last of the white wine? I asked.

He was sitting at the computer, and closed it up when I came in.

Why not, he said.

# THE CLUB

The best thing about the club was that it stayed open all night. There were other good things, of course, the poker machines, the beer being cheap, even the meals, but the never closing was what really appealed to Trevor. Even though he'd never made use of it. They'd have a few beers, and Lisa would be tired, especially now she was pregnant, and he'd have had a long day, getting up early in the morning in case anybody wanted to take a boat out, so they'd always go home, and he'd fall into bed and think, There goes another night, and I haven't tried out the round-the-clock opening. One day, he'd say, one day. It seemed to him that you might win in the middle of the night, that it would be a different time, and more lucky.

Of course it always looked the same. You could go in at half past eight in the morning and there'd be people sitting on stools, pressing the buttons, a beer in one hand, eyes focused on the machines, waiting for their pictures or numbers or whatever they'd chosen to come up. Trevor's mum hated the new pokies with the buttons, she reckoned there was an art in pulling the lever, if you did it in a certain way, with a certain touch, you could just about speak to the machine, you could persuade it that you were the winner, you should have the money. I've lost my magic touch, she said, but Lisa reckoned it hadn't made a lot of difference, she'd never won much anyway, but of course she didn't say that to Trevor's mum, it wouldn't have gone down well.

It was somehow dark inside the club, even though it was brightly lit, with lots of red, the carpet brightly coloured in red and yellow and purple, the machines glittering in black and gold and more red, and always the same noises, the clunking and whirring and occasionally the tinkling of a shower of money, when some of the players would pause and look up and sniff as though they could smell it, but others just kept on concentrating on their own pokie, keeping their wills fixed on it, not wavering.

Lisa wasn't drinking beer any more because of the baby, but she hadn't managed to give up smoking yet, not that it would have made any difference with everybody else in the place fagging away. She liked the bingo nights, they made it more interesting when you weren't drinking, and she always hoped she might win something, a side of lamb or a set of saucepans, a tray of cod pieces, a couple of chooks, a sandwich maker, nothing grand but useful, and sometimes she did, it made a big difference to the housekeeping. Trevor worried about money. Business was slow, especially in winter people didn't want boats, and Lisa was talking about giving up the job at the fish co-op; she only went a couple of hours a day but the money was useful. But it would get too hard with the baby, she said, might even be dangerous. All those heavy fish.

One night Trevor sat next to a man who got a terrific win, the money just kept pouring out. It was a two-dollar machine. Wow, said Trevor, though a lot of people didn't like you noticing. But this man smiled, and winked. It's all in the vibrations, he said. And again, later, there was the metallic pouring of money that just kept coming like rain in the tropics, and the man smiling. The next time he saw this man Trevor sat at the machine beside him, watching as he palmed each coin before inserting it. Another metallic shower. What do you mean, vibrations, asked Trevor. It's the machines, explained the man, who introduced himself as Tex. They like my vibrations, they pick them up from the laying on of my hands. Never fails.

Trevor bought him a beer and the upshot was that Tex agreed to transfer his vibrations to some of Trevor's money. About a hundred dollars in two-dollar coins should do it, he said. In return, just to prove he was above board, he left Trevor his Rolex, for the couple of days it would take. Trevor's mum laughed her rusty foghorn laugh. You've been diddled, she said, that's not a real Rolex, that's one of them cheap Hong Kong fakes. You're one sucker he'll never see again. And Lisa was furious, here he was giving a total stranger all their savings, they could have bought a cot and a basket and a pusher for that much. You wait, said Trevor, we'll get it back. A hundredfold, Tex had said, but Trevor didn't like to use a word like that.

A week went past, Trevor's mum cackled over the bingo and won a vertical grill that she gave to Lisa, and Lisa won a tray of rump steak which was handy. Then Tex turned up, with Trevor's money in a little cotton bag. Here, he said, try not to disturb the vibrations.

You going to count it? said Trevor's mum, but he ignored her. He put the bag in his pocket, didn't say anything. The women went yapping on, but he stayed silent. Took Lisa home early. Went to bed on the couch in the lounge room with his clothes on, and the alarm clock. When it went off at three o'clock he got up and walked through the empty streets to the club. It was brightly lit, with no one but the bouncer and the barman, dozing behind their counters. Trevor went to a machine, not thinking, letting it pick him, took out the bag, fished out the coins by their edges and fed them in. Pressed the button. Another coin, pressed the button. Nothing happened. The silence was heavy in the redness of the room. The bag of money was nearly empty. He'd never put so much in one machine before. He could feel only a few coins left. Feed one in, press the button.

The metallic shower began. Like a tropical downpour. Falling until the trough was full, spilling over. Trevor collected it all up into the little cotton bag, all except a fistful to use in the pokies again. But maybe they weren't the coins with vibrations, since they didn't ever win anything. And Tex never came back, so he couldn't get the vibrations done again. Though he did wonder how much help it was playing in the dead of night. Maybe when the baby came and woke them up in the small hours he'd try again.

## TELLING THE BEADS

I had a necklace. It was a new necklace when I got it, but its beads were very old. I imagined someone with lots of little trays of beads dipping into them, putting together pleasing combinations. Taking no notice of origins or ethnicity or history, caring only for the charm of the pattern.

Six of them are ancient glass, lost in water for a long time, smoothed, dulled, made opaque, with faint inner whorls and dints. Their colour is pewtery grey. When you put your tongue on them they taste salty. They have a cloudy denseness which is disturbing but very nice to touch, if you are one of those women who fingers your beads as a person chats to you. Is your attention more with your beads than with what I am saying? he thinks, for there is a certain vagueness, a certain inward gazing, in your eyes.

Standing in the bow of a boat, an ocean liner is the word for it, very high up, leaning on the metal railing; a child could slip through the gaps. But you stand hanging over the bar and gaze into the sea which is churned up by the screws and creams away at great speed, bubbling back into the ocean but making a line of white wake which shows you the ship's passage. It is possible to do this for lengths of time, staring down into the turbulent water, hearing the noise of the ship's engines muted by the churning and splashing of the waves it makes. It is so violent, this smashing of the water, and yet it is also very fine, like lace. It is mesmerising you, but you are thinking your own thoughts, with no children about that you need to stop sliding through. It's the tropics, warm, balmy, with faint airs caused by this movement through the water. Sometimes there are bands of phosphorescence. In the daytime flying fish soar through the air, dive under, soar again, their long firm silvery bodies cleaving air and water. They seem to be gambolling, but what would the watchers know of that. They think gambolling, because that is what it would be if they were doing it.

You always like to lean over the rail and watch the wake, even if it is a Manly ferry, or the lake cruise. You will never stand on an ocean liner again, and watch the tumultuous aftermath of its cleaving through the water. But that is all right, you have done it, sooner or later you have to stop doing things again.

You know that if someone falls overboard the ship will not be able to stop to pick them up. Its momentum is too great for that. It takes miles to stop a mighty ship like this. It will turn around and come back. If the person is a strong swimmer they may manage to collect him, but it's not likely. Perhaps if some quick-witted observer has thrown a lifebelt and he has swum to it. But most likely, that person is lost at sea. People used to sing hymns, a kind of prayer, *for those in peril on the sea.*

The necklace has fourteen small round carnelians, the red colour of pomegranates. Carnelian is a kind of chalcedony, and if you believe crystal lore it will encourage sensuality, be good for sex, protect against resentment, your own and other people's, and aid communication. People around the Mediterranean, in Rome, Crete, Syria, Egypt, were keen on carnelian, and used to make seals from it, because wax would not stick to it. Good fun, crystal lore, but surely pretty much nonsense. Not the part about the wax not sticking, that's fact. Making seals meant very fine and beautiful carving of the stone. Mine are not carved, they are perfectly round and smooth.

There was a woman here. She shouted Mum! Mum! Hello, Mum! What are those beads? They look like a rosary. Have you gone and got religion in here? She gave me a jab of a kiss. I don't know why she shouts. She has a kind of trumpeting laugh and she fiddles with me. Tucking in the rug, straightening my hair. Will I tweezer those whiskers out? she shouts. She'll do what she does. I never say anything.

We were in Italy, before we got on the boat. I bought some dress material cheaply and went to the village dressmaker to have it made up to a pattern I had bought in England, an Yves St Laurent dress, very plain, on a yoke, and ankle length. One lot of material was a kind of linen, and I had that made without sleeves, the other was a fashionable small flower granny print, in glowing dark colours, and I had that done with long sleeves. Splendid dress, a man on the boat said, and patted my knee. The dressmaker worked in a sort of basement room, opening through a big arch to the street. It wasn't underground, but it was probably originally a barn for animals, and then perhaps a workshop. It was cavernous and very cold, even on the Ligurian coast the weather was cold. She heated it with a *bombola*, which was a giant gas bottle in a kind of wheeled cradle, with a jet of flame coming out of it and spread by a mesh mantle that glowed red with the heat. When I took my clothes off to try the dresses on she would move it close to me and I would shuffle away. It reminded me of the gas bath heaters of my childhood, that people would light and jump back from when they roared into flame. Geysers they called them, not a comforting name. Quite often people had their eyebrows singed off. I never heard of a *bombola* exploding but I was only in the village for a month. And couldn't read the local newspapers. I didn't see why it wouldn't explode, all that gas pouring out into a naked flame. The woman laughed and made jokes, and I would smile because I didn't understand them. She made the dresses beautifully; we communicated perfectly successfully over those. I think sewing for this strange foreigner—the *Australiana*—gave her something to talk about. She liked talking and laughing. Her workroom was a constant party.

There are silver beads on the necklace, three large and two small, the large one the centrepiece, with striations down them, like excessive longitude lines, they bulge at the equator. There are four plainer ones, octagonal, leaden in colour with points rubbed shiny. They are not very expensive silver, it's the kind you get in India, or in Persia or Turkey, often in necklaces with amber, or turquoise. I liked the carnelian, a bit unusual and I used to be a person who looked good in red. With my dark hair. That is what people said: with your dark hair. It was shoulder length and very dark, very smooth and curving under, with a deep fringe; when my father saw this style for the first time he said, Ah Cleopatra. I was pleased by that.

This shouting woman. She takes my hand and shakes it. Quite gently, she means to. Do you know what you are doing with these? she says. I shouldn't think so, but I look down at my hand since she is shaking it. These beads are small, dull, brown and round like seeds, all the same, and yes there is a cross on the end. I don't think I know what they are doing there. Did someone give them to you? she shouts. Do you want to talk to a priest? I raise my eyes to her and stare at her. I can tell she makes up conversations with me. Shouts something, then imagines what my answer might be, and tries to come up with some sort of reply to that. You never were a Catholic, she says. We none of us were. But who knows, at the end . . .

The woman who is always here comes in, and the shouting woman asks her, in a normal voice more or less, Do you think she is getting religion, sister?

The woman says, I see no sign of it—the woman in the next bed gave her the rosary. She likes to have it round her hand. More like worry beads, I'd say. And why not, the shouting woman says. She turns to me and raises her voice: Well, see you later, Mum. In a couple of days I reckon. Look after yourself.

She kisses me again, and goes off waving. I look at the rosary. The little cross thing looks silver but I bet it isn't even Indian silver. Base metal, I reckon.

The dining room in Cambridge had tall windows, with shutters, looking over the park, the house was Georgian, the room very large and stuffed with bookshelves, all the French books were kept there, their covers dun coloured so it was an effect of rather dreary wallpaper. I used to take one out at random and check that the pages had been cut; I remember French classes and the embarrassment of the hiss of cutting pages, it was a sign you hadn't done your homework, but on those shelves I never came across one that hadn't been cut, so I suppose they had all been read. The dining table was enormous, and when I needed to help the children with their meals I had to stand up and lean right over and even so I could not quite reach, they had to push their plates nearer. The table the Professor said had belonged to the Vice Chancellor of Hong Kong university. This seemed a curious fact. Once we had some friends from Australia for dinner, we were eating chicken that I had bought from the game shop in the market and it had lead shot in it, and we made all sorts of jokes about the English shooting their chickens for sport these days, releasing them in the woods and hunting them down, and laughed ourselves silly but then somebody said maybe a fox had got into the henhouse and the farmer had been shooting at that and hit a chicken. Plausible, I suppose. Bill picked up an ornate fork which was part of the only set of cutlery we had to eat with, sculpted and etched with arabesques and flowers, a bit fancy for my liking though obviously very handsome but I prefer a more Scandinavian plainness, and he remarked that it had the head of Minerva on it. What does that mean? I asked. It's real silver, he said, the French standard, not quite so high a count as sterling, but very nearly, only a small percentage below. He was on the way to becoming a rich lawyer and so knew these things. You mean, I said, that this is practically sterling? Real silver? Oh yes. Quite old, too.

It would have been from the Professor's marriage, in 1939, to a rich bourgeois lady. Maybe not new then. The head of Minerva gave me a bad fright. If I'd known I would have counted them every time I used them, expensive irreplaceable heirloom silver. I should have guessed from the weight, but I had not even considered. The kitchen was skivvy's Georgian, the sink terrazzo, the draining board ancient smelly wood, it had dark crannies; I spent as little time in the room as possible. What if I had already lost some? Still, I was grateful I had found out, in future I would check every time.

Later, I counted them, and there were twelve of everything, so presumably that was all right. I did think that Madame the Professor's wife might have told me. The silver was not unlike that in their house in the Paris suburbs, but that was plated, I knew, I'd looked at the marks. EPNS they said.

So grand, that Georgian house was. Five storeyed, the rooms large and gracious. At the back it looked over a college garden, with lots of daffodils in green green grass. The children were happy there, in their room on the fourth floor. I took them to school, along the frightening narrow pavements of Drummer Street, filled with red buses crawling halfway across them, it being their terminus, down little streets to the thoroughfare of Jesus Lane and into a small street called Park Street. They liked school, though the lunches were hard to take; once they had liver with mashed swede which left them not quite speechless with horror. There was a famous kitchen shop called Scurfield's in Jesus Lane, which I had read about in Elizabeth David. One day on sale I bought a large copper bowl, hemispherical in shape, for beating egg whites. You do them by hand with a big balloon whisk, and they rise and stiffen magnificently. I made excellent cheese soufflés with such egg whites. A soufflé is a fine dish, it is flattering, people are impressed with your skill and grateful you are lavishing it on them, but it is actually very economical. And I never had a failure. This sounds like a boast, but it was actually because of taking care, following the recipe precisely and being very careful not to get any of the yolk into the egg whites, for then they will not whisk up. It is because egg yolk is fatty, it spoils the chemical effect. As the copper bowl aids it.

The last kind of bead on my necklace was made of ceramic, and quite long, more than two centimetres I think. I am never very good with metric, it doesn't have the logic of imperial. They are coloured in a dark brownish-blackish-purplish colour, much like certain aubergines, with patterns of white running through. They are all the same, but different. They would have been made in the same pattern, but during the firing the white lines and dots would have melted through differently. Someone told me they are eye beads. Tibetan, she said. They are only vaguely eye-like, not like the ones in Turkey which are bright blue and have distinct eyeballs in them. I bought several keyrings made up of bunches of these but they were very flimsy, the eyes were made of blown blue glass and the loops by which they were attached were blown glass too, so the first time I used them nearly all of them broke off and fell on the floor of the car when I turned the ignition on. Blue glass eyes turned up in odd places. Evil-eye beads people call them, but they are not that exactly, they are to protect you from the evil eye. My daughter bought a handsome ceramic one, on a plaited string. I used to look at it and wonder if it had saved her from anything. My ceramic ones are more impressionistically eyes, and the more beautiful for that. They might be Egyptian; I think the provenance of my beads is generally Mediterranean. There are six eye beads; as you can see, everything is even and so symmetrical, except for the extra silver longitude bead that centres the necklace. You could put it together from my telling you these beads, work out a pleasing pattern to make from them, as did their maker, dipping into her trays of varied beads, choosing only for beauty, not for meaning. Except I haven't told you about the clasp. It is a very large hook and eye, made of brass, the eye a large O, almost big enough to be a thumb ring, the hook shaped like an anchor or a fishhook, both of them apparently cut by hand out of a thick flat sheet of brass. Of course your necklace, even though the beads were the same, would not look exactly like mine; they would be siblings, not identical. My words can tell you a lot, but not everything.

The necklace was a birthday present from my sisters. It was expensive, the three of us shared the cost. I don't know where it is any more.

# A SCENT OF GERANIUMS

I keep marvelling at this unexpected bliss. When you are eighty-five bliss is really something, and unexpected bliss even more so. I think my life has been quite lucky, not so much in obvious ways; anyone looking back over it would not be at all likely to think, how lucky. But I do, because I know what it might have been. But bliss: there hasn't been a lot of it.

Bliss is my little granddaughter Ellie. Unexpected in her existence. I was not young when her father was born, was of an age where I thought children were not something that would happen to me, and neither was her father young; I didn't believe he ever intended to be a father. And here I am, at this really quite old age, with a lively little two-year-old in my life. Not as much in my life as I would want, but I am greedy for her company; I see her quite a lot, it's just not enough.

Of course it's a cliché, that people get so much more

pleasure out of their grandchildren than their own children. People keep saying, the lovely thing is you can give them back. I think the lovely thing is you can just enjoy them. You don't have to worry about how they will turn out, their natures, their characters, their manners, their nourishment; their parents can do that. I remember the work of it, and how there wasn't much time for play. Whereas with my little Ellie play is what there is. Play, and contemplation. I sit and gaze at her. Your own child is nature but a grandchild is a gift.

It helps that she is beautiful. Of course all grandmothers think this. But Ellie truly is. She has hair the colour of French butter, large blue eyes, dark lashes, a mouth like a rosebud, flawless white skin with flushed cheeks. What a cliché, you'll be thinking again, and so she is, she is the perfect Victorian image of the angel baby. The sort that often seemed too good for this world, and sometimes ended up under a headstone that said so. Those heartbreakingly comforting things Victorian parents told themselves when their babies died, how God wanted her for one of his angels, and so took her to heaven, where they will see her again one day. Too good for this world, needing to move on to the next. That protective habit they had of not calling them by name until it was pretty likely—though not certain—they would survive. I remembered reading *Seven Little Australians*, oh not as a child, that was not my childhood, where Baby is a little girl of four, and the new baby is called the General, still not a given name.

It seems that I am not superstitious; I am not afraid to think of my angel granddaughter in the context of dead babies. She is very much alive, and likely to remain so. I rejoice in her beauty, though I do think of Yeats: *only God, my dear, could love you for yourself alone, and not your yellow hair.* That was in a poem for Anne Gregory. I said to Ellie's father, my son Oscar, remember Yeats' poem for his daughter, where he hopes she will not be too beautiful, and Oscar said what are you talking about, how can a woman be too beautiful? I looked the poem up: *May she be granted beauty and yet not Beauty to make a stranger's eye distraught*. Later on the poet says: *Hearts are not had as a gift but hearts are earned.* It comes down again to love. It's all to do with Yeats having known beautiful women who did not care, who got things too easily and didn't value them. Especially did not love him. Oscar of course has not read Yeats, he insisted on having a boy's education, science and the mechanics of things. I don't think Ellie can be too beautiful, he says to me, however could that hurt her? I emailed the poem to him and he said, It's very time-specific, isn't it. Those things don't apply now. Whereas I think that is the point, they do, in their way. A poetical way, perhaps, but that is how it is true.

He thinks I am old, and do not know things. Even when I wasn't old he thought I didn't know things. Though I was never young, in his life. Now I know a lot, and I have my marbles. They are maybe a bit worn, one or two of them cracked, possibly chipped, but they rattle together very satisfactorily, and shoot true when they have to. I like to think they were of the finest agate when they began. As was my education the finest. My father was a stern man, and austere, his obsession was politics, that was all the conversation at home. I found Yeats for myself but it wasn't his politics that I cared about though he had plenty. Nineteen twenty-five I was born, and in England; my parents had been astute enough to get out of Austria and make a comfortable life in England. Imagine, all through the thirties, the conversations in my house. Not games or play, and I have thought, perhaps not much love, or anyway not much expression of love, but respect, and care, the sober virtues. It is actions that speak, they would have said.

My skills were in languages, German of course I spoke like a native as we used to say, and by the end of the war I was working for the government; secret stuff, it was then, I suppose it isn't now, six decades and more later. After the war I spent a couple of years with the British in Germany, and then I came back to England, and married Rudy.

We believed we were in love. We chose one another, but the reasons I came to learn were murkier and more complicated than sexual passion. There was plenty of that, at first, and I believe I was quite pretty but not so beautiful as to think he loved me for my brown curls and not myself. And anyway I knew that brown curls however shiny are not yellow hair. He was from the east, Poland. I knew the war had damaged him but not at first how much. I thought I could love him and heal him, but I couldn't. He taunted me with my failures until one day I answered back. Then I understood that while he did things to break the marriage and I put it back together we could continue, but when I took my turn at smashing it was doomed. We got divorced.

This may seem a pale account of violent events and it is, I know it is. Over the years I have carefully washed away the pain, the anger, the bitterness, the sadness of love lost, till now it is a simple faded scrap of fabric, and better like that, it can't hurt like that. I went to work with refugee groups; languages are useful in such cases, and there are always refugees. I worked on my own, self-contained, practical, kind, but also remote, so my powerlessness couldn't hurt me. I understand the condition of refugees, being one before I was born, and then coming to this country in my middle age. Of course I know that what I am here is an immigrant, not a refugee. Safer, but not always easier.

I am looking after Ellie today; she is asleep now, she has a sleep in the afternoons, she loves it, a funny little girl to love sleeping, very wise I find it, she curls up so happily with her favourite toys. I imagine she has good dreams. That would be a prayer for a daughter, that she will always have good dreams. When she wakes up she sings to herself. When I go in she is rosy-cheeked and tousle-haired, the perfect angel child. But such warm and living flesh. Now she is sleeping and I am sitting on the balcony and reading poems I have read before.

I like to read poems so I have them in my head to think about instead of remembering things. Ellie makes me remember things, about Oscar, and his father, and Rudy, they can get too hard and then I like to pull out T.S. Eliot's lilacs, the woman taking one from a bowl and twisting it in her fingers saying to her friend, ah, he does not know, he does not know, the man is young, he does not know what life is, he who holds it in his hands. Well, what's new in that? Or Gerard Manley Hopkins' aspens, all felled. Though you have to be careful because sometimes they join the memory instead of replacing it and make it worse. *It is the blight man was born for, It is Margaret you mourn for.* That was barbed, that was. I am not Margaret, but just for a little there I could have been. Start mourning for yourself at eighty-five, you will come to a bad end. Margaret after all is a child. A little autumnal grief is good for a child. I am waiting my moment with Ellie. When she wakes up I will recite it to her; she won't understand but she loves cadences. *Margaret, are you grieving Over Goldengrove unleaving* . . . She will sit and watch intently as I speak the words, with all their music.

I am not Margaret. I am Gretta. Close enough. But you can't substitute Gretta for Margaret. *Gretta are you grieving Over Goldengrove unleaving* . . . you turn it into bad doggerel.

I sit in Clarice's orderly apartment. Oscar (named for my father; I do have my pieties) likes everything just so, and married a wife of the same mind, which is why I thought they might like the bit in Yeats' prayer for his daughter where he hopes her bridegroom will *bring her to a house Where all's accustomed, ceremonious*; for that is Clarice's housekeeping, the large spaces well-kept and adorned, and the little girl always exquisite; fresh, clean, scented, so it is a joy to pick her up and smell her, hold her close and inhale the essence of her. I remember people used to remark of a woman, *She keeps her kiddies something lovely*, and so does Clarice keep Ellie, but then the child is also naturally fastidious I think. Her mother's daughter, of course. Though Clarice is dark, and so is Oscar; his father was the fair one. I sit reading; when Ellie is about I gaze at her, but on my own I like to read, read not think. I don't think when I'm watching Ellie, I contemplate her, that is enough.

I had no intention of marrying Oscar's father. I had done marriage. It was a sweet little affair, that would run its time, end in an equally sweet regret. But then, I got pregnant. At my age. Like a green girl. I had got used to the idea that children would not be my lot. I wasn't going to tell him, but he guessed. Made an honest woman of me. That was his joke. Just as well; I imagine how cross Oscar would have been to have a single mother. Custom and ceremony, that's what he likes. Just as well for Oscar; not so much for me. So I thought. His father was a good man in an affair, not so good in a marriage. I missed my freedom, but can I blame him for that? It was the child who took away freedom. And then he died, when Oscar was eleven, the sorrow of his son's life, if not of mine. Yet I still think of him, with gratitude, and a certain sadness; Oscar likes to think I mourn him. I wonder has he ever worked out the closeness of his birth date to my wedding date? I have never asked, nor told him; I am inclined to lie about the year I got married. Having done it, I think it is a good idea to make it work really well. Make believe I was a virtuous wife when I conceived my child. How old-fashioned these ideas are. Who cares now? Sometimes I look at young women, not needing a husband to have a baby, and envy them.

But really, I envy no one. I have my granddaughter.

And Oscar is clever, in his way. I think he probably does know the exact dates. Just as he would never say he did.

I can hear Ellie singing. I go in and she gives me one of her brilliant smiles. She can climb out of bed herself which is lucky, as she is very heavy for an old woman to lift. I was old enough to be her father's grandmother and now her father is old enough to be her grandfather. I ought to be a great-great-grandma here. The ways of the generations are mysterious. She wears pyjamas even for her afternoon nap; this is one of Clarice's rituals. Pyjamas mean sleep, they are a message Ellie hears. So now I have to dress her; I let her choose. We are complicit, Ellie and I. This morning we went round the corner to the café and I had coffee; Ellie had a babycino. I know Clarice doesn't approve of this, though I can't think why, the babycinos there don't have marshmallows in them, like some, they are just frothy milk. Ellie knows this disapproval and doesn't mention babycinos to her mother. This is as it should be, grandmas and granddaughters should have their secrets. Sometimes at my house I give her a little orange juice, freshly squeezed, of course; she calls it chewy juice because I leave a lot of the pulp in. She doesn't have juice at home. It goes without saying, no sugar. No cakes, no fancy biscuits. Greek yoghurt, no sugar or fruit or flavouring. She likes to eat broccoli. What a little paragon she is. But given to small outbursts of rage, not exactly tantrums, since they pass quickly. When her will is thwarted unbearably she goes rigid, shakes her fists, lets out a yell. I find these rages very moving. She wants to bend the world to her way, and is overcome with frustration when she can't. She will learn; that's necessary. But also sad. Part of me would like her to remain unreconstructed.

She has chosen a blue dress with a pattern of leaves in it of an acid green colour, quite pale. A sophisticated dress, the blue the colour of her eyes so it suits her. She gets sick of pink, she tells me. She is wearing sandals with little leather flowers across the straps. For some moments she bends over to watch her feet walking in them, with satisfaction. She loves her body, plump and sturdy as it is, it is hers, it doesn't occur to her not to enjoy it. I expect she will stretch, one day, grow long-legged and slender like her mother. For now she is chubby and gorgeous. Clarice sometimes doubts, in these times of preoccupation with obesity: is she perhaps too fat? I stroke the bracelets on her arms and legs. No, she is perfect.

You look at a baby and wonder why God made ageing. If there is a God. Ageing would suggest there is not. *Age and decay in all around I see.* Of course this is a hymn begging God to help us, and equally of course he doesn't.

We go out on to the terrace. It is spacious, naturally, and with fine furniture. Around the edge are tall troughs of geraniums in splendid bloom. Ellie isn't allowed out here on her own, and Clarice is nervous about her being here with me. I tell her I am still quite quick on my feet, and Ellie is a good girl, she knows what she is not allowed to do, at least when someone is watching her. The flower troughs make it difficult for her to get very near the edge anyway.

Mobs of geraniums shout scarlet. I might think them vulgar but they can't be. Clarice doesn't do vulgar. Still I don't care for them much. Though they are cheerful. Ellie puts her hand up to them. She's not allowed to touch them, and doesn't, but a small heap of petals falls on the ground. She looks at me in horror. All the ones on the ground are yours, sweetheart, I say.

She goes inside to get her tea set. I bought it for her, at an antique shop, it's painted tin, Victorian, not used at all. Maybe it belonged to one of the angel babies who went to heaven before she grew old enough to play with it. Sad thought. Makes you hope baby angels have tea sets. It's very pretty, all over roses. Not geraniums. The geraniums blaze in the sun. There is a shelf of herbs too, rocket, chervil, thyme, basil; pots of basil. *Isabella and the pot of basil* . . . with her murdered lover's head buried in it and causing the herb to flourish. The flower troughs look like sarcophagi, those narrow ones you see in ancient chapels.

What is it Eliot says? Something about the corpse you planted in your garden last year, has it begun to sprout, is it going to bloom this year?

You can see why I need to read, or gaze at Ellie. Where is she? Isn't the tea set taking a long time? I'm on my way to look for her when she comes, carrying the little basket I got for it, it didn't come in its original box, I don't think I could have afforded it if it had. She's thirsty, so we get glasses of water and bring them out to have a picnic on the terrace. Ellie—I think Clarice would prefer she be Eleanor, but somehow that doesn't happen, and her mother is gracious enough about it—collects the geranium petals and puts them in one of the pretty tin teacups. She is pressing and squashing them with her fingers, trying to turn them into pulp. Soup, she says. Delicious soup. They quickly go mushy. She puts her nose to the cup, wrinkles it a bit, passes the cup to me. Smell? she says.

I do. I pick up the cup, hold it in front of my nose, and take a deep snuff. Ah. I have to sit down quickly in a chair. The instant passing of more than sixty years can wind you like that. I am twenty again, the war is finishing, we have come to Belsen, the concentration camp, we are not the first in but soon after, people everywhere, dead and alive, dazed and limp, so you can't tell which, and there is a smell, it seemed familiar. I said to a woman whose eyes looked in mine, What is that smell?

She said, The scent of geraniums?

Ah, yes, I said, the scent of geraniums.

It is the smell of death, she said. Her voice was barely a breath.

I looked at her. She was all eyes and bones. She put her skeleton hand on my arm, briefly, a whisper of a touch. It was her eyes that held me. She was wearing those clothes they called pyjamas, the uniform of the camp. I squatted down beside her. The smell of death, she said. We have become used to it here. She looked at me with those eyes and I settled down beside her. I knew she wanted to tell me her story, she believed she was dying and she wanted someone to know it. I don't know how I knew that, but I did. Maybe at twenty, you can still know by instinct.

She told me her story. It was the first of such narratives I was to hear. Later, they became almost generic, the hiding away, the Nazis coming, the parting of families, loved ones dragged in opposite directions, watching elderly parents killed, clutching the baby daughter while the elder child and husband were marched away, the filth and the crowding in the railway train, the daughter dying before the camp was reached, the mother saying, I was glad, she was spared worse fates.

The elements of the narratives like cards in a pack, and people dealt different combinations. But not very different. Still greasy slippery stinking cards. Only a few suits, this hand or that hand, but all in the end the same.

The woman saying, My little girl, my baby. She was so beautiful, her cheeks so round and rosy, and still so when she died, I was glad she was beautiful when she died, not worn away, I remember her eyes were round and puzzled, but not suffering, I don't think they were suffering. She wouldn't have looked like that if she was suffering.

The mother's face squinted up but there were no tears, I thought she was dried up of all tears.

I'd spent a quarter of my life in a country at war, my parents talked politics all the time, discussed what they knew, what should be done, how Hitler might be stopped, the fate of Austria, of Poland, but I had not heard a story like this. She was a woman from the country that would have been mine, had not my father's good management saved us. Luck, you see, I said I was lucky. The woman told me her story and I listened, dazed. She said, I wanted someone to know. You are my witness.

Yes, I said, I will keep your story. I will look after it. I held her dirty hand, its bones barely encased in skin, so delicately, while I tried to press comfort into it.

Did I say I would tell it to others? I don't know. I didn't tell it. I married Rudy, who had a story very like hers. I did keep it, locked away until the smell of a flower I have not cared for and had little to do with, indeed must have avoided, opens it up to me, six and a half decades later. On a cool terrace in a city far away, with a child I hope will never know except as a faraway tale such narratives of dread. I think, I should write this down, the story of the scent of geraniums in the concentration camp of Belsen, told to a girl of twenty by a woman only a little older, but ages, ages deep in pain and loss and suffering. I have looked after the story, hidden it safe away, but a story needs telling.

I don't know what happened to her. I think giving me her story might have been the last thing she did, that she kept herself alive for that moment. She was carried away, I didn't see her again.

The geranium petals are sticky and smelly in my fingers. Ellie has got bored with flower soup. I notice a sound I have been hearing, the scrape of wood across tiles. She is at her favourite job of moving furniture. She has pushed a chair across to one of the sarcophagus troughs, climbed up and is standing among the geraniums. I move so swiftly; eighty-five maybe but I can move if I have to. I grab her before she reaches out to the railings of the terrace, ready to topple the three floors to the ground below. I pluck her out, clutch her to me, kiss her neck and cheeks. She struggles, has one of those moment's rages, beating her fists on my chest, and I put her down.

If Clarice had seen this! It would be the end of me as child minder. I would be lucky if I ever saw my darling again. As it is, how shall I explain the geraniums crushed by her strong little body? Look, I say to Ellie, oh poor flowers, all squashed. We must try to make them better.

# LETTERS FROM EDEN

*Dear Mama,*

*Here it is, the long promised letter, after such a bombardment of postcards. I know you will understand there has been such business settling in that not a moment was spare for writing a real letter. And of course I wanted you to see the beauty of this place, and the postcards so clearly show that. You have perhaps been thinking that they are a little false, that they cheat, but not at all, so far from that: they do not do justice. The sea is at least of such a blue, the bays so seductively indented, their slopes as charmingly terraced, the buildings just such graceful affairs of porticoes and cupolas.*

*I intend to write you of our doings, since I know you are interested, and I confess I do it a little for my sake, so as to have a record of our life here. You remember, when Nazlyn was first offered the posting, we wondered, we had heard so little of the place, it seemed so remote, so far away down almost to the Antarctic, and not exactly a significant player on the world stage. Australia, and its capital Eden. Ostensibly a promotion, but Nazlyn was not sure; more money, and seniority, yes, but was it likely to be a furtherance to his career? But of course what matters is the serving of our own beloved country, so of course willingly we came.*

*Ah, but we shall be happy here. The inhabitants are a friendly and cheerful people. They have a habit of referring to their country and its capital as 'the best kept secret in the world, eh'. This ending a sentence with* eh *is a linguistic trick of theirs; not exactly a question, more an invitation to agreement. You know how excellent our English is—our foreign service would not send us abroad unprepared—but we have had to take a little trouble to adapt to the dialect. The children have dived deep in; they now have broad Aussie accents. You hear them playing in the garden with the local children, their voices ring out through the sun-drenched air, you cannot tell them apart.*

*I send you my love, dearest Mama, and that of all the family. I do miss you, and the beloved country of my birth, which in my mind is always so pure, so white, so cold. But at least when we represent it overseas like this we bring it with us; where we live is always a little piece of our own dear fatherland.*

*Your affectionate daughter,*

*Sirimenet*

*Dear Mama,*

*Today I shall tell you about our house. As you know, our country and Australia have been friends for a long time, so when the capital was established here ours was one of the first to take up an embassy, and so it has one of the finest positions in the city.*

*I should tell you, Eden is a planned capital, a willed city, its site chosen; built as the result of a competition in the early years of last century. It has a fine harbour, one of the deepest in the world. The Australians are a sea-regarding people, so this siting on the coast was important to them. So was establishing it in a place that was neither Sydney nor Melbourne—the capitals of two of the original colonies that federated to form the new country—but halfway between the two. The wife of the man who won the competition was responsible for the idea of the buildings; she drew them fastidiously on gold silk, and part of their beauty is their femaleness: a lot of breast-like cupolas and fine delicate lines in even the most grand of civic buildings. They are open and welcoming and at the same time sheltering. There are colonnades, and most marvellous narrow canals—somewhat Moorish, I venture—feeding into pools of water, both a delight in this severely hot weather which I am growing to love. I saw myself always as the happy native of chilly climes but this sun is seductive, especially observed from the cool shade of the sea-breezy colonnades.*

*Eden was originally a fishing village and the locals eat a lot of food from the sea, it's their staple diet, along with vegetables and a very fine series of goat cheeses made in the hinterland; the terrain is quite rugged, so goats and olive trees flourish there. The oils are very fine, made with the same care and discrimination as the wines further inland. The people flourish on this diet, are tall and slender but well-made with strong bones and clear eyes. They are keen swimmers and have sporting regimes which are second in importance only to their arts activities, of which more later.*

*When they want to eat red meat it is kangaroo. I wish you could try some, it is passing fine, lean and full of flavour and enhances gamey sauces. They don't have beef, whose hooves would destroy the delicate terrain of this ancient country. There are wild pigs in the woods—the bush they call it, though it be full of trees—which are hunted, and turned into superb prosciutto-like hams.*

*The children send their love, they are growing brown and wiry, soon you might not recognise them.*

*With love,*

*Sirimenet*

*Dearest Mama,*

*I realise I have described the city but not our house. It is its own version of the ubiquitous porticoed and colonnaded architecture, having that diversity in harmony which makes a city like Paris so beautiful though of course this aesthetic is entirely different. Our house is built on terraces above a small sandy beach where we all swim, sometimes in the company of dolphins. We have a jetty and a boat. Picnics in gardens or in nearby bays are the popular form of entertainment. Even in winter I believe the sun shines warmly, and though there are cold sea breezes there are sheltered spots where you can bask.*

*The house is, naturally, large, with French windows and floors of polished wood or local stone. The furniture is a mixture of the style of our own country and of native pieces. There are great forests about here and the trees are harvested for their beautiful woods and made into graceful furniture, its own very contemporary style but somehow you can imagine Chippendale or Hepplewhite in this day and this place finding a similar idiom. There are local textile industries too, cottage industries I suppose you'd call them, using mainly hemp which is woven into coarse and fine fabrics that fall gracefully, and demonstrating the decorative skills of the first peoples, the Aborigines they call them, who practise weaving and tie-dyeing and painting techniques of great finesse and subtlety. I am making a collection of such textiles for myself.*

*The style of these houses is such that they do not need air-conditioning. They catch the summer breezes and are cool and shaded, alive with the noise of water in the narrow canals running through courtyards. In winter they're warmed by solar heating which I gather is very cosy.*

*It is all so different from home, is it not? I know you will want to picture how we live. It would be wonderful if you could come and visit. And Nazlyn at the right moment will make some discreet inquiries. Of course it is quite likely that it won't be possible, but it is a nice thought. The children often speak of you.*

*Your*

*Sirimenet*

*Dear Mama,*

*I am sending you pictures the children have drawn of their school and their friends there. I am sure you will recognise Amy and Sam and Guido and Despina should you happen to meet them! They are keen that their grandmama should know all about it. Of course you know how anxious we were, coming from the best education system in the world, about what we would find here, but it is going well. They start school at 8.30 am and work academically during the morning: two foreign languages, plus Latin and later Greek, literature in English and in translation, grammar, mathematics, sciences. There is what is called little lunch of fruit and yoghurt at 10.30, then a light but nourishing dinner at 12.30. After that quiet time: a nap for those who choose it, specially the younger ones, reading, a short walk, really anything they like so long as it is solitary and silent. Then it is time for the arts. I did not expect we would find the equal of our country in this respect, but I have to say the Australians value such things immensely. Music, both listening and performing, painting and sculpture, theatre, writing; the children are encouraged to develop their talents across a broad spectrum of activities. Excellence is encouraged, but most important is participation.*

*The second part of the afternoon is given over to sporting activity, either swimming or running or more structured forms of games and gymnastics. Again the emphasis is on each child finding where his skills and proclivities lie.*

*Twilight lasts late in the summers here, we are quite far south, and there are long days full of fruitful activities. The children flourish under this regime. Already they are mapping out paths for the future. Ren plans to be a writer, and not just because novelists here are such highly valued members of society; he has always had a desire to put the world into words. Valli is devoted to dance; of course she is young, this may change. Yes, I know you will hardly recognise their names. The Australians have an endearing habit of abbreviating the names of their friends. It was something of a shock to us at first and we maintained their formal given names, but now the affectionate diminutives have come to delight us. So: Ren and Valli—I cannot quite say, your new grandchildren.*

*Eden it may surprise you is quite a small city, compared with the ancient and mighty metropolis that is our capital. This is because the government has avoided much in the way of bureaucracy and indeed you might wonder how it functions but it does seem to. Of course paying no attention to a military does help. Australia says that like New Zealand it is a small country on the edge of the southern ocean, what should it have to do with military might? The arts community is probably larger than the bureaucracy: the symphony orchestra, the various chamber groups, the theatre companies, the National Library and the National Gallery, the Museum, the Schools of Art and of Music, and of course the university itself; these, with fellow diplomats, make up our social acquaintance. Entertaining is informal, often involving the out-of-doors, or festivities on the great colonnaded terraces which I realise are a nod in the direction of the old colonial architecture when homesteads were protected from the heat by deep verandas. Often there will be some impromptu artistic performance occur. These people like nothing better than to sit with a glass of their excellent wine and listen to a poem written for the occasion, or a piece of music, or to join in some dancing. I think it must be their schooldays training in both performing and following artistic endeavour; nobody feels at all threatened by such manifestations. Of course they are of high standard which always helps.*

*So you should picture quite a vigorous small community but spread around the shores of Twofold Bay, all the little inlets and indentations providing water access to the population. Water travel is a favourite means of transport; small fast ferries link what otherwise might be far-flung suburbs, there are always plenty of water taxis, and many people have their own boats. Dolphins like to disport with these boats, and even the tightly scheduled ferries will take a moment to play with them.*

*Your loving daughter,*

*Sirimenet*

*My dear Mama,*

*I notice I have not described the political situation. You will find it quite curious. There are several political parties—yes, indeed—and every four years an election. At this time there is much excited political debate, I believe, each party accusing the other of all sorts of bad behaviour, corruption, evil-doing—* Keep the bastards honest *is one colourful slogan—then one party is elected and things settle down exactly as they were before, since everybody is really quite happy with the way the country runs and has in the end little interest in changing it. All workers are generally organised into unions to negotiate terms of employment and these seem to be amicable; neither employers nor employees have much interest in changing situations that so evidently function well. The Prime Minister has a most charming house on one of the headlands, much like ours really, possibly a little larger; he holds open house, wine and nibbles (that's their word for the delicious little snacks that accompany drinks) in the garden every other Tuesday, when the people can come and talk to him about . . . well, anything, it seems. More likely a new book of poems than politics; there is a charming habit of writers always presenting a copy of each new book to the Prime Minister which pleases him greatly; he was most enthusiastic in telling Nazlyn of this, he had to keep fetching books and reading extracts. Of course he is a poet himself. There is always a comfortable party, never a crowd.*

*I embrace you.*

*Sirimenet*

*Dearest Mama,*

*I do confess I am and am not surprised that the children's drawings have not reached you. I am aware that wise censorship is one of the exactitudes that have made our country great. But I am not sure why that should be necessary here. Perhaps they appeared to be in code. Never mind, the children think that you have got them, and that will have to do, for now. I shall tell them how pleased you were.*

*Love,*

*Sirimenet*

*Dearest Mama,*

*Perhaps you will be as amazed as I am to realise we have now been here more than a year and a half. We have had our second winter. Winter here of course is something of a joke for a happy denizen of our chilly climes like myself. Winter, I say. Where is the snow? Where is the ice? The frost? Look how the sun shines nearly every day. The locals reply in shivery voices, But feel the bitter winds straight from the Antarctic, and it is true there are occasionally cold breezes and sometimes storms when the ferries skip and cavort across the wind-blown waves, but generally this season is in its own way benign.*

*There is a suggestion perhaps of a voyage home to our dear father country. But we shall see. Perhaps after Christmas. Of course here it is not the same as our wonderful celebrations against the cold, but I have to confess that I was quite amused by the languorous summer festivity, the fish and prawns and oysters, the cold wine, the hot sun and swimming in the cool crystalline waters of the bay, or the lively waves of the ocean beaches. Christmas is the long summer holiday, and the children spend more time in the water than out of it. Waking time, I suppose I mean.*

*My love,*

*Siri*

*Dearest Mama,*

*I expect you will find my news quite shocking. I have been offered a job. Yes, women here work after marriage, and even when they have mothered children. I would begin in the new year. Teaching our language at the university; there is a lively faculty of literary and linguistic studies which is keen to employ my services.*

*But the children, you will say. It will only be in the morning, there are no lectures in the afternoon. All businesses and institutions are well equipped with crèches, and university students who all have scholarships and pay no fees (this country believes that the education of its young people is its most valuable asset) in return help with the afternoon sporting activities of the younger children, and this socialisation of what you might call grown-up children—the students—with the small ones is seen as valuable for both.*

*You may find it difficult to understand, but I am tempted to accept it. You know I was quite an intellectual before my marriage, and though of course within this context my mind and all my faculties have been fully extended, nevertheless this seems such an interesting chance to disseminate the language of my beloved country. A tiny addition, you might call it, to Nazlyn's work here. Yes, I think I must take it.*

*Ren and Valli send love and kisses . . . and so do I.*

*Siri*

*Dear Mama,*

*It is a worry that you have not been well. I know you say it has passed but I am concerned about anaemia, it is never to be dismissed lightly. Plenty of red meat, that's the most important thing, and here is a nice morsel of news: Australia's kangaroo meat will soon be available to you. Yes! It is a negotiation Nazlyn is most pleased with, this trade between our two countries. So keep a watch for it at the end of the month, I think it will set you up well. Remember, do not overcook it, it must be eaten very rare.*

*I think of you, and send my love . . .*
*Siri*

*My dearest Mama,*
*This will probably be the last letter you will have from me. I cannot say anything here. It is better that you not know anything. Please be sure of that, you do not know anything. And further to that, believe nothing that you hear, not announcing that of course, keeping your own counsel. One day it will be clear and until then you must trust. Be certain: this is a good thing for us, that our belonging is here now. Remember, we are happy. That is what you must keep hold of: that we are happy. And not forgetting that I am your daughter, loving as always, and behaving as you have always taught me to behave, passionately doing the right thing. You must believe: all will be well with us.*
*Sirimenet*